THE GIRL WHO WASN'T THERE

ALSO BY PENNY JOELSON

I Have No Secrets

ALTERNATIVE TITLE: GIRL IN THE WINDOW

THE GIRL WHO WASN'T THERE

PENNY JOELSON

Cover design by Kerri Resnick
Cover image © Derek Adams/Arcangel
Internal design by Ashley Holstrom/Sourcebooks

Published by Sourcebooks Fire, an imprint of Sourcebooks
P.O. Box 4410, Naperville, Illinois 60567-4410
(630) 961-3900
sourcebooks.com

Originally published as *The Girl in the Window* in 2018 in Great Britain by Electric Monkey, an imprint of Egmont UK, Ltd.

Library of Congress Cataloging-in-Publication data is on file with the publisher.

Printed and bound in Canada.
MBP 10 9 8 7 6 5 4 3 2 1

For Cherry

THE GIRL WHO WASN'T THERE

There's no one coming to look for me because
no one even knows I've gone missing.

—*Unrest*

No one sees me. I am a ghost. I am invisible. Life for me stopped still, one day—when I was not expecting it. Out there, I know that life goes on, that time moves forward, but it does so without me. I know I shouldn't, but I want to look once more—to take a peek out through the window at a world that is not mine. Do I dare?

1

It's dark when I see her. I'm closing my curtains, ready for bed—and there's a woman hurrying along our street toward the bus stop. There's something intense about the way she's moving. She darts like a bird. It's as if she's rushing to catch a bus—but there's no bus there and no one waiting. The street is quiet. I'm not sure why I keep watching but I do. She's skinny—with long, dark hair, maybe in her late teens, early twenties. She's barely more than a silhouette in the darkness, but as she passes the streetlight, it casts her elongated shadow across the road. The glow highlights the long, thin cardigan she's wearing. She pulls it tight around her, head bent against the chill November wind, but she goes past the bus stop without slowing down.

I see her glance around briefly as two cars pass. Now a silver car's coming. It swerves and stops alongside her. Her head turns sharply. At the same moment, a man jumps out from the passenger side. He grabs the woman by the arm. She pulls away. They're struggling. At least, that's what it looks like. Within seconds, he's opened the back door of the car and she's in. He bangs the door shut and jumps back in the front. The car drives off, disappearing around the corner.

It happened so fast—but I'm certain she didn't want to get into that car. The man was dragging her—forcing her in. I think he even had his hand over her mouth. I can barely believe it. I keep replaying it in my mind. My heart is thudding like a bass drum.

I'm staring out at the now empty street, still in shock, when a movement catches my eye. I look up at the house across the street, the window opposite mine. The curtain moved, I'm sure it did. Someone was looking out. Did they see what I just saw?

Should I call the police? There's a couple in that house across the street—if one of them saw, maybe they've gone to call the police right now. But even so...

"Mom!" I yell, grabbing my phone. "Mom!"

She's watching TV downstairs, and I don't think she heard me. Anyway, I don't need her to tell me what to do, and I shouldn't wait. I shouldn't let them get too far away.

I sit on my bed and dial. My hand is shaking. I've never done this before—never dealt with a real emergency. I ask for police.

There's a calm voice at the end of the phone—a man's voice. He listens and then starts asking me questions.

I give my name, *Kasia Novak*, and address, *47 New Weald Lane*.

"Did you get the license plate number?" he asks. I feel instantly devastated. Why didn't I?

"I'm sorry. No. It was all so fast," I tell him.

"Don't worry—you did the right thing to call. Any information you can give us will help. Can you describe the car?"

"It was silver—a hatchback... I'm not sure what kind."

I can describe the woman but I didn't see the driver and only have a vague impression of the man who jumped out. I'm a useless witness.

"Silver hatchback," he repeats, as if he's writing it down. "We'll get someone on it right away."

"Oh, and I think someone else might have seen it—across the street," I tell him. "I think there was someone at the window upstairs. They might even have called you, too. It was number forty-eight."

"We'll speak to them. Thank you for reporting the incident. Please call us if you remember any other details." He gives me another phone number and a case number, which I write on a scrap of paper.

I have a sinking feeling as I put the phone down. I wish I'd gotten the license plate number. Maybe whoever was watching across the street did. I hope so.

"Mom! Mom!" I call again. She still doesn't hear. I want to tell her. I need to tell her. I stand up, holding on to the window ledge for support, and then walk slowly out into the hallway, one hand pressed against the wall. My glands are throbbing in my neck, and my legs are throbbing, too—a constant dull, familiar ache. "Mom!" No reply. I clutch the banister and put one foot gingerly on the top step. I've been thinking about trying to go downstairs for a few days, but I know now isn't really the right moment. I'm too shaken up on top of everything else.

"Kasia! What are you doing?" Mom appears at the bottom of the stairs, looking up at me with concern. My legs give way, and I sit down on the top step.

"I was calling you. You didn't hear. I thought I'd come down..."

Mom's up beside me now, tutting and holding out her arm. "You look very pale, *mój aniele*, my angel. Come on, time for bed. How many times do I have to tell you to take it slowly, not do too much too quickly? Just getting out of bed is a big achievement. You're clearly not up to trying the stairs. You should text me if I don't hear you."

I'm too tired to argue, but I want to prove her wrong. I'm so fed up with being in my bedroom all the time. Tomorrow, I think to myself. Maybe I'll try tomorrow. But I still want to tell her what just happened.

Mom helps me into bed and sits on the edge as I tell her all about what I saw. She's really shocked.

"Kasia, how awful! Are you sure?"

"I think so..."

Mom touches my hand gently. "You did the right thing to call the police. Now settle down and get some sleep. You look exhausted."

She goes back down and I lie in my bed, staring at the same four walls. It's been ten weeks since I've been downstairs.

2

I'm sitting by my bedroom window, waiting for Ellie to come over after school like she promised. She's the only one of my friends that still does. The street is busy with cars picking up kids from school and kids walking home. It looks so normal, it's hard to believe what I saw last night actually happened. I've been playing it over in my mind all day. It feels like a bad dream, not something real. Where is that woman now—what happened to her? I wonder if someone has reported her missing.

I glance at the house across the street. Have the police spoken to them yet? Was someone looking out last night, or did I just imagine I saw the curtain move? At the bus stop, groups in school uniforms stand talking. A toddler in a stroller has pulled off one shoe and is chewing it. I watch as she takes the shoe out of her mouth and flings it under the bench. Her mother is sitting staring at her phone and hasn't noticed.

The bus comes, blocking my view, and when it pulls

away, the people, including the woman and the stroller, have gone, but I can still see the purple shoe sticking out sadly from under the bench.

A man in his twenties with dark hair and glasses arrives at the bus stop and kicks at the shoe curiously. I start making up a kind of Cinderella story, where the man takes the shoe and puts a photo of it on a Facebook group, and the woman comes forward gratefully to claim it. Turns out they're both single, and when they meet to hand over the shoe, it's love at first sight.

I see a police car coming along the road, and it pulls into a parking spot farther down the street. Does this have something to do with last night? At first I think they want to ask me more questions, but the officer walks quickly up to the door of number 48. I watch eagerly and see the front door open. The officer talks to a woman, and I can see her shaking her head.

Once the door closes, the officer knocks on the doors of the houses on either side, but no one is home. Then he crosses the street. He's coming here! The doorbell rings. I wish I could run down and answer it, but I have to wait for Mom to do it. I hear her talking to the officer, and I wonder if she'll bring him upstairs, but she says goodbye after only a minute and then comes up.

"What did he say?" I ask eagerly.

"They haven't found out anything about an abduction,

Kasia," Mom tells me. "No one has been reported missing, and no one else contacted them about it. He said the people at forty-eight saw nothing. They were both downstairs watching television."

"I thought someone was there, watching," I say, "upstairs—in the room across from mine. I saw the curtain move, like someone was peeking out."

Mom shrugs. "The police are looking into it. If there's anything to discover, I'm sure they'll find it."

Mom goes back down, and I'm still waiting for Ellie. Where is she? I'm suddenly worried she won't turn up. I'm dying to tell her what I saw. Maybe I should have texted her, so she'd know I had something to talk about for once.

Just when I think she's really not coming, I finally spot her, hurrying along the sidewalk, her ponytail bobbing up and down. I can see she's trying to be quick, but it feels like a hundred years before she turns into our gate and rings the doorbell. I hear Mom's footsteps on the hall floor as she goes to let Ellie in, and then more, lighter steps as Ellie pads up the stairs. She comes into my bedroom with a beaming smile and two plates of Mom's apple cake. I take a deep sniff of the delicious cinnamon smell that has been drifting through the house, making my mouth water.

"Sorry I'm a little late—it's all been happening today!" she says, plonking herself on the edge of my bed and handing me a plate.

"Tell me!" I say. I like hearing what's going on at school. It makes me feel more part of it, although it also sometimes makes me sad.

"At lunchtime Serene got into a fight with Bethany," Ellie tells me. "A real fistfight—Bethany pulled Serene's hair and a whole clump came out! I saw it in her hand! It was over some boy. I don't even know who."

I feel a pang. I hope it wasn't Josh. He's a boy I like who's a year older—a boy with ocean-blue eyes and a husky voice. I can't imagine him with Bethany or Serene, though.

"Then," Ellie continues, "Dimitri and Rafi were messing around in math class, and Mr. Treaker completely lost it and slammed a ruler on the desk so hard it flipped in the air and hit Serene in the face! She had to go to the nurse's office and now she's got a huge black eye, too!"

"Poor Serene!" I exclaim, though I can't help laughing.

"We shouldn't laugh," says Ellie, who is giggling, too, "but she's always so obsessed with how she looks—and I'm sure she started that fight!"

"Anyway, listen," she says, when we've both finally stopped laughing. "I have news you're going to want to hear!"

I want to say, "So do I!" but she's made me curious. Her eyes are shining, her smile even broader. It must be something good, really good.

"What?" I ask. I take a bite of cake and lean forward. "What is it?"

"Guess," she says. "It's about you..."

I hesitate. For one moment I wonder if it's something to do with Josh. Maybe he asked about me...

"I can see your dreamy eyes!" she teases. "No, it isn't about *Josh*, Kasia!"

"Okay." I feel myself blushing. Ellie knows me too well. "I can't guess—you'll have to tell me."

"You're going to love this!" she insists, stuffing too much cake into her mouth. "Oh, your mom makes the best cake!"

"Tell," I demand, rolling my eyes because now she can't speak.

She swallows and grins at me.

"Remember that story you wrote—that one that was like a mash-up of *Hunger Games* and *Titanic*?"

"Sort of. That was long ago—before I was sick. What about it?"

"It was sooooo good—Miss Giles said she might enter it in a competition. Do you remember?"

It's weird thinking back. I first became sick in June, so it must have been May when I wrote that story. I remember the noise in our English class and the way the room fell silent as I started to read my story out loud. I remember even Rafi and Dimitri had their eyes fixed on me as I read. They clapped at the end, along with everyone else. Miss Giles was full of praise, saying I could be an author one day.

But that was months ago, when we were all in ninth grade.

Now my classmates have moved up—they are sophomores, with a different English teacher. I don't even know which classroom they are in or what time the lesson is. I'm taking tenth-grade classes, but I don't feel like I'm in the same year as them.

"Kasia?"

I realize I haven't answered her. "Yes," I tell Ellie. "I remember."

"Well, listen to this... She *did* enter it—and you won! First place!"

"*What?* You're joking!"

"Look—here's the proof."

Ellie scrabbles in her backpack and pulls out an envelope that has already been opened. It's addressed to Miss Giles at our school. She slips the letter out, unfolds it, and hands it to me, pointing.

"See—First Prize awarded to Kasia Novak."

"Wow!" I say. I've never won anything before in my life—except a tiny rubber duck at a festival when I was five. It used to glow in the dark.

"Miss Giles is so excited," says Ellie. "She came running up to me in the corridor."

"What did I win?" I ask, scanning the text. I'm hoping it's money, though I know it's unlikely to be much. With Mom not working, every little bit helps.

"You get to go to an award ceremony in a theater," she tells me. "Oh..."

Her voice falters and she looks at me, her hand covering her mouth.

"When and where?" I demand.

"It's not until February—and it's in central London somewhere. Maybe by then..."

I'm conscious of my throbbing glands, and my heart's pulsing, too. I feel weak but I also feel a surge of determination. I look Ellie in the eye and tell her, "I *will* be better. I can't miss something like that! And I'm going to get back to school, Els."

"Have you been downstairs yet?" Ellie asks.

"No, but I'm going down for dinner today. Don't tell Mom—she doesn't know! I want to surprise her."

"Really? That's great!"

Ellie's being a supportive best friend, but I can see she still looks doubtful. She knows how long it is since I've been downstairs.

We read the letter again, together. I still can't take it all in.

"Oh, look, you get a gift card for books and a selection of books donated to the school," Ellie tells me.

"Miss Giles will be happy about that!" I smile.

"Look, I've got to go," says Ellie. "Tons of homework. I'll try and come again on Thursday."

It's only after she's gone that I realize I forgot to tell her about last night.

3

My words to Ellie may have sounded brave and determined, but I know it's not going to be that easy. I am not in the same classes with all my friends but, back in September, I did try to be. Nobody knew I was going to be so sick for so long.

I remember Ellie waiting for me at the school entrance, a beaming smile spreading across her face when she spotted me.

"I'm so glad you made it!" she told me. "I didn't want to start the new school year without you!"

"Same here," I said, waving Mom off in the car. I meant it, too. I'd always been determined to get well by the end of summer vacation. I knew that I wasn't okay, though. I was achy, weak, and in pain. I'm sure Mom knew it, too, but we both wanted to believe that once I was in school, I'd feel better and everything would somehow, magically, go back to normal.

"Come on, let's go in," said Ellie. "Don't want to be late on the first day!"

We walked to the main entrance. I felt so weird and

wobbly, as if the ground underneath me was moving. I tried to ignore the dull ache in my legs and the swollen glands making my neck stiff and uncomfortable.

Inside, everything seemed different. The corridor looked so much longer. Erin and Tilly rushed up to say hi, and Tilly tried to hug me. It hurt, but I didn't want to say so. They were clearly happy to see me back, chattering and asking me questions.

"I thought it was just tonsillitis," said Erin. "How come it took you so long to get better?"

"The doctor said I had post-viral fatigue," I explained. "I still felt sick even though the infection was gone. No idea why. It just happens sometimes. Did you have a good summer?"

"We went camping in France," she told me. "The first week was amazing, but then it rained the rest of the time! I never want to go camping again."

She kept talking, telling me about all the other things she'd been doing. I zoned out. People were talking all around me, too. I couldn't take the noise. School never used to be this loud, did it? As we reached the stairs to our homeroom, I looked up and was overcome by panic. It was a flight of stairs—a flight I'd climbed every day for years, but now it looked like a mountain. How would I ever get up there? And the crowds—I couldn't stand all the people swarming around me. I suddenly felt so fragile, as if I was a delicate flower about to be trodden into the ground.

"You are okay, aren't you?" Ellie asked.

"Not really," I told her.

"You can use the elevator if you need to."

I did, but I felt weird, embarrassed, standing waiting for it. The elevator is for disabled students. I'm not disabled. When I got out on the first floor, I was sure everyone was staring at me.

I sat down with relief in my homeroom, listening to more vacation stories, with people coming up to say they were so happy I was better and how I looked fine. I didn't feel fine, even sitting down. When I looked at my class schedule, I had a sinking feeling. I even asked Ellie, "Have they added more classes this year?" and she looked at me like I wasn't making sense.

"French first!" she said cheerfully. "Look, we've got Madame Dupont! She's the best."

I like Madame Dupont, and I like French, but I didn't smile back, because the room was on the other side of the school. The thought of having to stand up and walk down more corridors, packed with students, already felt like too much.

I made it to French, but within minutes I felt so sick I couldn't sit any more—I had to lie down. Ellie took me to the medical room. The nurse called my Mom right away.

I'd lasted thirty-seven minutes in class.

Now, I stand at the top of the stairs, looking down. I imagine I'm an Olympic skier at the peak of a challenging slope. The previous contender has been taken off in an ambulance. I don't know the extent of her injuries but, after checks, the organizers have declared the course safe. I am not so sure.

I cling to the banister, aware that I am holding my breath as I put one foot tentatively forward. Then the other. I'm getting into a rhythm, but halfway down I feel light-headed, and my legs feel like they're going to give way. I haven't been downstairs since that day—the first day of the semester, September 2, when I tried to go back to school. But I am starting to improve.

When I didn't get better after tonsillitis, Mom and Dad were constantly trying to get me to do more, and I had to make them understand that I couldn't. Dad actually thought I'd gotten lazy from being sick in bed. Mom thought it must be depression or anxiety, especially when she took me to the doctor, who did blood tests that all came back clear. The doctor said it was possible I had post-viral fatigue, and mentioned chronic fatigue syndrome or CFS, though it's more often known as ME. It stands for myalgic encephalomyelitis. That was probably the reason I was taking so long to recover. But I don't think Mom and Dad realized exactly what that meant, or how long it might take. I didn't, either. I know now, though.

I. Know. Now.

People can be sick for years with this. Some people never get better. I'm not going to be one of them. I can't.

I've been thinking about trying to come downstairs for a couple of weeks—but I've been so scared of getting stuck halfway, or not feeling well enough to go back up again, that I've been too frightened to even try. I know I have to get over this fear, but it's based on real experience. I only have to do the smallest thing, and it wipes me out completely. Already I need to sit down, but that's okay. Now it is as far to go back up as it is to keep going, and down is definitely easier.

I start going again, before I panic. And then I've made it! I'm down! I'm a little giddy, but I'm here.

I wait for a few moments to get steady, then I take a deep breath and stroll casually into the kitchen. I'm almost surprised that it looks exactly the same. I feel like so much time has passed that Mom might have a new tablecloth or kettle or something. She's busy at the stove, stirring something in a saucepan. The smell is like a life force to me. I feel stronger just being close to it.

"Hi, Mom! That stew smells delish."

She nearly drops the spoon in the pan.

"Kasia!" She rests the spoon on a plate and flings her arms around me. She knows to be gentle. She lets go of me and rubs her eyes.

"Don't cry, Mom!" I tease.

"It's onions, just the onions," she says with a smile. "You should have told me you wanted to try coming down. I would have helped you, *mój aniele!* Do you feel okay? Are you sure it wasn't too much? Come—sit. After all those stairs, you need to sit. Let me get you a drink."

She brings me a cushion for the hard, plastic chair.

My whole body is so sensitive these days. I'm already starting to feel weak, but I don't say anything about it. I hope Dad gets home soon. I'm not sure how long I'm going to last.

I glance at the photos on the fridge. Me and Dad making silly faces, Mom posing on a bridge, a picture of my aunt and uncle in Poland. There's one missing—the one of me and my brother Marek. I'm sad, but not surprised. Dad and Marek haven't spoken since he dropped out of college and went traveling around Europe.

Dad is home early, to my relief—and the expression of delight on his face as his large frame and bald head fill the kitchen doorway makes it all worthwhile.

He's still in his work clothes, dirty from his day at the building site, but he does his funny version of a traditional Polish celebration dance in the small kitchen. Mom hastily moves pots and pans out of the way so nothing goes flying, and I am laughing so much it actually hurts.

"*Moje kochanie*," he says, gently stroking my hair. "It's so lovely to have you down here and not exiled upstairs. I hope this is a sign of good things to come."

"I only wish Marek was here to see you, too," Mom says, sighing.

"So do I," I tell her, getting a pang as I imagine my brother here, too, grinning and high-fiving me.

Dad tuts scornfully.

"Dad!" I protest.

"Let's not spoil the evening talking about *him*," Dad says firmly. "Give me two minutes to get changed and when I come down, we'll talk about something else, something happier."

Mom winks at me when he's gone and picks up her phone from the counter. "I'll take a photo of you at the table and we'll message it to him," she says quietly. "Marek will be so pleased."

Dad comes back down and Mom serves up. "Well, what's new?" Dad asks.

"We had a visit from a police officer," Mom says. "He was very handsome!"

"I hope he didn't stay long, then," Dad teases. "This about what you saw the night before, Kasia?"

I nod and Mom tells Dad what he said.

"I hope they find the woman," I say. "I just want to know she's okay."

"Well, you did the right thing reporting it," Dad says to me. "The rest is up to them."

I know Dad's right. There's nothing else I can do.

"I thought we were going to talk about happy things," says Mom.

"Hey, yes! How about this for a happy thing?" I say, smiling.

I tell them about winning the writing competition, and they are both thrilled. Dad gets up to do another celebration dance, but Mom tells him to stop or he'll get indigestion.

"I want to get well enough to go the award ceremony," I tell them. "And I want you both to come with me."

"I'll do my best," says Dad, "but you know how things are. It isn't always easy for me to get time off. It's a big project, this assisted living facility, and we're a month behind already. Hopefully by then we will be back on track."

Although I want Dad to be there, I'm glad that he's not even questioning the idea that I'll be able to go myself.

"It's exciting, Kasia, but you need to be careful," says Mom. "We'll have to see how you are closer to the time."

Mom may be more realistic, but I prefer Dad's optimism. However, as she speaks, I realize that the room is starting to spin. I don't want Mom to be right, but, in the end, I have to tell her. "I need to lie down."

"Let me help you back up to bed," she says. "You've done really well, but that's enough for now. I can bring you up dessert if you'd like some."

As I stand up, panic rises in my chest. "Mom—I don't think I can do it—I don't think I can get back upstairs. I need to lie down now!"

"Lie on the sofa for a minute," Dad suggests. "Here, take my arm."

He helps me into the family room, where I collapse on the

sofa. I still feel like I'm on a boat in a storm and the panic is overtaking me. I want my bed—I want to be in my room.

After twenty minutes, I don't feel any better. Dad sits down beside me.

"I want to go to bed," I tell him.

"I'll help you, *kotku*." He holds out his arm.

I shake my head. "I can't stand up, Dad."

"Lucky you have a strong father then," he says. He's standing now, smiling and holding out both arms.

"Dad!" I exclaim. He hasn't carried me anywhere since I was about five years old.

"I've carried heavier things around the site today," he assures me. "Look at these muscles."

Before I can protest, he has me in his arms and is lifting me. As much as I hate being treated like a child, I enjoy feeling safe and warm and held, and I am more grateful than anything when he lowers me gently onto my bed.

4

I can't get up the next day or the next and, apart from crawling to the bathroom next to my room, I don't try to do much else. The only other thing I stand to do is draw the curtains—open in the morning and closed at night. I know Mom would do it, but I want to look out—remind myself that there is a world out there.

This evening, I look across the street, and I can see a light on upstairs in the room opposite mine at number 48. Someone is drawing the curtains there, too. I briefly catch a glimpse of the figure, but it doesn't look like the man or woman who live there. It's someone skinnier—a girl, I think. Was it her I saw in the window the other night, when the woman was abducted?

Now that I've been downstairs, my small bedroom is feeling even smaller than it did before. Lying in my bed, all I can see is the pale pink walls, painted when I was six, matching pale pink curtains, my wicker chair by the window, and a white desk and white bureau against the wall. On the wall is a small picture—a Polish village scene with a girl outside a church—that once belonged to my grandmother. And I have a tiny bedside shelf for my glass of water, phone and clock.

My duvet cover makes my room look more grown up—it's silky pink with splashes of purple on it. There's no room for my cello in here, and maybe that's for the best. It's downstairs in the corner of the family room, and I am glad not to have to look at it and be constantly reminded that I can't even pick it up, let alone play it. Marek's room is a little bigger than mine, and Dad asked if I wanted to swap when Marek went to college. But I didn't—his room is painted black and orange, which would have taken many coats of paint to cover. And anyway, I didn't want to think of Marek as having left home. I thought he'd be back for summer vacation, and even when he'd finished college. I'm glad his room is still as he left it, waiting for him to come back.

I lie in bed, sleeping, listening to podcasts and audiobooks on my phone, meditating, and thinking of ideas for stories. Then my mind turns to Josh. I like him so much. Only Ellie knows how I feel. I wish I'd had the courage to say something to him while I was healthy. I kept hoping he'd speak to me, but maybe he's shy. He's in the grade above me but we were both in the orchestra—I could have said something then, but I didn't. He's probably going out with someone else by now and I wouldn't blame him. He has no idea how I feel about him, so it's not as if he'd be waiting for me to get better.

I get a message from Marek. He's seen Mom's photo of me sitting downstairs, and his message is full of excited smiley emojis, along with a photo of a frozen pizza, with the caption "My job is cheese sprinkling!"

Dad had better not see that!

I reply, telling him about the writing competition, and get more excited smiley emojis back. I think about telling him about the abduction, but I'm too tired to text that much.

I lie back and think about the award ceremony again. I just have to get well enough to go. I *must*.

A few days later, I'm feeling a little bit better. I don't feel like attempting the stairs again, but I'm mostly okay being out of bed. I sit on the floor and open my chest of drawers, just for something to do. There I find the get-well card with the cheerful yellow sunflowers on it. I open it and run my finger over Josh's signature. I wonder if he ever thinks about me now. The card is also signed by the other twenty-four members of the orchestra, but his is the only name in there that really matters to me. He's an amazing violin player, and when we'd finished orchestra practice, he used to meet my eyes sometimes and smile. I'm sure something would have happened between us one day.

I put the card back in the drawer. My legs are hurting from sitting on the floor, but I don't feel too bad otherwise, so I stand stiffly and sit on my wicker chair by the window, looking out. I still feel like I'm on a boat—but it's a gentle rowing boat now. I watch as the woman at number 48 comes out, bumping the gray stroller with a rain cover over it, down the steps to the street. She hurries off up the road, and I glance up to the window above. There's no one there.

It's raining heavily now—big drops streaking down my window like bars, reminding me of the prison my room has become. It's hard to see through the rain, but I try. There's no one looking out across the street. Cars splash past in the big puddle by the bus stop.

The haziness makes everything seem unreal. It's like the rain is trying to wash away what I saw—washing it all away, wiping the slate clean, a fresh start.

I can't remember it clearly now. Maybe none of it happened at all. But if it *did*, what happened to that woman? I can't help wondering about her.

It's a week later when I get up the courage—and have the energy—to go downstairs again. And it's fine! I stay for a whole meal, and also get back upstairs by myself, too. I do it again, each day stretching it out a little longer, and I don't have any ill effects.

I feel full of hope—I'm finally getting better—and I want to do more.

Mom comes into the living room, waving a package at me. "I'm just running next door," she tells me. "The deliveryman left it here this morning, when he couldn't get anyone to sign for it."

"I could take it," I offer.

Mom looks at me in surprise. "Are you sure you feel up to it?"

"It's only next door. And it would be good to get outside. Let me, Mom. I'll be fine."

"Okay," says Mom, but she's looking very doubtful.

"Is it forty-three?" I ask her. "Won't they be at work?"

"No—forty-seven," says Mom. "Mrs. Gayatri."

"How did she manage to miss a package?" I comment. "She never goes out."

"She does sometimes," Mom says with a shrug. "Maybe she was having a nap or just didn't hear the door."

"Okay. I won't be long," I tell Mom.

It's weird putting on outdoor shoes when I've worn nothing but slippers for months, and I've rarely been out of bed enough to even need them. My shoes feel hard and uncomfortable in contrast.

"Put your coat on," Mom fusses. "And your scarf."

"It's only next door!" I say, but I do it anyway.

I take the small package and step out of the house so happy to actually be outside. I wonder what Mrs. Gayatri has ordered. It's rectangular but not heavy. We don't see our neighbors very often. There's a young couple on the other side, at number 43. We only know their names because they sometimes have packages delivered while they're at work, and Mom takes them in. I don't remember Mrs. G. ever having a delivery before, though.

We don't see her much, either, though I used to sometimes see her weeding her front garden. She's the only person around here who has pots and flowers and bushes in the front. She's not very chatty, but she always has a smile and says hello if we pass her. Of course, since I've been sick I've only seen her from my window, on her rare walks up the street to the store.

The cool breeze makes my cheeks tingle as I stand on Mrs. G.'s front step and ring her bell. I feel a buzz of excitement and breathe in deeply. It's one step closer to normal life. There's no answer, and I wonder if the bell is working. I wait a few moments, try again, and then resort to the old-fashioned lion's-head knocker. I listen but can hear no sound from inside. The lion's face is snarling at me, and I'm about to turn around and go back home because my legs are beginning to throb, which sometimes happens when I'm standing still. Then I hear a small sound—a definite movement from inside. "Mrs. Gayatri?" I call. "It's me—Kasia from next door. I have a package for you."

The door opens, and Mrs. Gayatri peers out nervously. She seems more shrunken and wrinkled than I remember, but her eyes are soft and kind.

She smiles. "Hello, dear. I haven't seen you for a long time. I wondered if you'd gone away to college."

"No. I'm fifteen."

People often think I'm older because I'm tall for my age. I have Dad to thank for that. Mrs. G. is short—shorter than me.

"I've been sick—I *am* sick. It's ME—Chronic Fatigue Syndrome," I tell her. "I get exhausted after I do anything."

"How awful for you," she says.

"This is the first time I've been outside for months," I tell her.

"Goodness, is it really? You poor girl! So, what can I do for you?"

"I've just come to bring you this." I hold out the package. "The deliveryman left it with us. I'm sorry—I can't stand for very long, and I have to get back now."

"Thank you, dear," she says. "It's nice to see you. And if you ever feel like a change of scene—or company—you are welcome to pop in. And I mean that."

I nod and smile. I always thought she liked keeping herself to herself. She doesn't seem to have many visitors. But there's a look of longing in her eyes as she says, "I mean that," and I think she is genuinely lonely.

"Everything okay?" asks Mom as I come back into the house. She's standing by the door, and she gives a big sigh of relief. She's clearly been waiting for me, worrying. I made it. I went next door to deliver a package and came back again.

"Don't make a big deal of it, Mom," I beg.

"It's progress, Kasia—progress," Mom says softly.

I nod. I am mega happy with myself, though I'd never admit it to Mom.

Back upstairs, I rest in bed for a while and then go and sit by the window. A few people are walking down the sidewalk, each in their own separate world, though they are only a few feet apart. A man on his phone, a woman with fashionable high-heeled boots, a teenage girl with a bobble hat. A silver car appears and slows down near the girl. There's something weirdly familiar about the scene, and my heart skips a beat as I remember the abduction. Is this the same car I saw? Is it going to happen again—to this girl? I am frozen to the spot.

The car pulls over and parks, and a man gets out. He glances toward the girl. I hold my breath. She's still walking. She hasn't noticed the car. Fear rises in my throat—but the man is walking the other way.

He's heading for the barbershop on the corner. He goes inside.

I look again at the silver car and realize it isn't the same kind. It's a two-door and a completely different design.

My eyes turn to the upstairs window at the house across the street. The curtains are closed, and there's no one there—but then I see one curtain move. A hand—a face—dark eyes, looking out. Then nothing. Again, I didn't see clearly, but I'm sure it's the same face I saw before, and I'm even more certain now that it wasn't the face of the woman who lives there. This face is narrower, younger. A girl. Who is she? She disappeared so quickly.

The couple have a baby, but I've never seen a girl go into or come out of that house. If she's the one who was looking out of the window, then why did the woman lie about anyone else living there?

5

"Mom, did you know there's a girl living over at number forty-eight?" I ask. "As well as that couple and their baby. I've never seen her go out. Don't you think that's weird?"

"A girl? I haven't seen a girl," Mom says as she picks up an empty mug from my bedside shelf. "Are you sure?"

"Yes," I tell her.

I start watching the girl's window more closely. I'm certain she's real. A couple of days later, I see her again, just as I hear Mom coming up the stairs. I call her urgently. I want her to see the girl—to prove that she exists. Mom comes running, thinking something's wrong.

"Mom—look! She's there now! The girl!"

I only turned away for a second, but as Mom reaches the window and I turn back, the girl has gone. Mom peers across the street. "I don't see her, *mój kotku.* What's so interesting about this girl?"

"I think it was her," I tell Mom. "I think she was the one

who saw what I saw, when that woman was dragged into the car. And the police didn't speak to her, did they? Should I call the police again and tell them?"

"But the police went and talked to the people in the house, and nobody saw anything. You know that," says Mom. "If a woman *was* abducted, I'm sure someone would have missed her by now and reported it. They found no one missing, did they? Maybe you were mistaken?"

I shake my head. "I know what I saw—and there is a girl across the street. I've seen her, too. And I never see her go out."

"Someone could say the same about you," Mom comments.

"Yes. Maybe that's it!" I exclaim. "She could be sick like me—and that's why she doesn't go out. Maybe the people across the street didn't want her stressed with questions, and that's why they didn't mention her to the police?"

"It's possible, I suppose," says Mom. "If unlikely."

"I want to go across the street and ask them," I tell Mom. "Maybe we could even be friends?"

"Oh, Kasia. I don't want you going around there annoying them. If you really think this girl exists and she might be stuck inside, sick like you, then maybe I could go over and ask for you."

"Would you, Mom? Thanks! That'd be great."

Mom goes downstairs and I sit at the window and watch her cross the street to number 48. It's the man who opens the door. I can see Mom talking, but she isn't there long.

I wait eagerly for her to come in and back upstairs. "So?" I ask. "What did he say?"

"Well, I asked—you saw me. And the man had no idea what I was talking about," she tells me. "I felt embarrassed, Kasia."

"What did he say?"

Mom gives me a quizzical look. "He said there's no girl there."

"What? Did he speak English? Maybe he didn't understand," I say, bewildered.

"He had an accent, but his English was clear enough," says Mom. "Perhaps you imagined her. Or maybe a girl *was* there and now she's gone, I don't know. But she isn't there now, and I think you should focus on other things."

I go and lie down on the bed—but I can't stop thinking about it. I don't understand what's going on. The man must be lying—but why would he? I'm sure I saw her! Only glimpses I know, but why would I imagine it? If only she wouldn't always vanish so quickly...

As I think more, prickles start running up my spine. And then I start having, what some people would consider, truly crazy thoughts, like, what if the reason she vanishes so quickly and that no one else has seen her, not even the people who live there—what if that's because she's...a ghost?

Today I looked out of the window—even though I know that I should not—and I was shocked. I saw the ghost of myself—looking back at me. A girl in the window opposite. She peered out, just as I did, her shadowy shape a mirror image of mine, though her hair was light, her face pale. Is she a ghost, just as I am? Is the whole street maybe full of ghosts like me, and we know nothing of each other's plight, or why we can neither live nor our souls rest in peace?

6

I look out of the window as often as I can that evening and the next day, but she doesn't reappear. Then, in the evening, I see the woman coming out of the house. She's on her phone. She walks up past the bus stop toward the store, barely glancing left or right as she crosses the street.

She's deep in conversation with someone, and I can't help wondering what they're talking about. Maybe she's telling a friend how the house gives her the creeps—especially that small front bedroom. She gets a chill every time she's in there, and it makes her shudder. She wants to move.

I know this is just my imagination running wild, but as I watch, the woman turns and walks back to the house, still speaking in an animated way into the phone. She isn't going anywhere—she just came out to talk privately. Maybe she was nervous about speaking in the awkward atmosphere in that room. She can't tell her husband. He'd think she was lying.

And she can't explain it, but she feels as if she's being watched. She looks like she's shouting into the phone now.

She's so loud I can hear a little of it, but I can't make out the words, and, anyway, I don't think it's English.

The woman is back at her front door now. She glances up in my direction as she takes a key from her pocket, and she sees me. I pull back from the window, embarrassed, partly about being seen and partly because of the story I've been making up. I wait a minute and then cautiously look out again. She must have gone inside.

The ghost theory keeps going around and around in my head even though I try to ignore it. I don't think I believe in ghosts, but right now I can't think of another reason why I keep seeing a girl who nobody else sees, not even the people who live there.

When I feel up to it, I ask Mom to bring me my tablet so I can do some research. I can't spend too long on it or I get headaches.

I start by looking up the address, 48 New Weald Road. Maybe I can find out who lives there, or even if anyone has ever died there. I don't expect to find anything, but at least I'm doing something.

The first Google entries are real estate pages, house prices and homes for rent and for sale. Then there are the stores, the hairdressers. There's a report on a burglary at number 249. A bus route being diverted. I keep scrolling through pages. It's very boring, and my head soon starts to hurt, so I stop.

I lie down and decide to try meditating, which a doctor said might help me. Mom wasn't impressed with the suggestion, but I found I really like it. I have an app on my phone, and it is definitely relaxing and something I can do without effort. Mom is baking downstairs. The smell wafts up, and I start by visualizing a piece of cake in my mind, focusing on that and nothing else.

Thoughts keep drifting back, though, even as I try to let them go. Maybe I need to think of another way to research, like asking someone who knows the area. I wonder if Mrs. Gayatri could help—she's lived here a long time.

"I was thinking I might go next door and visit Mrs. Gayatri," I tell Mom next time I'm well enough to be downstairs.

Mom glances up doubtfully. "Are you up to it? And I'm not sure you should go bothering her. I think she prefers her own company."

"Maybe that's because she doesn't have any other option," I suggest. "Anyway, she invited me—when I took that package to her. She sounded like she really wanted me to come."

"Okay, if you want to." Mom smiles. "Don't stay too long, though—you don't want to tire her, or yourself, either. Here—I'll give you some apple cake to take with you."

Like last time, Mrs. Gayatri takes forever to come to the door.

"Another package?" she asks, looking puzzled. "I don't remember ordering anything."

"No, this is some of Mom's apple cake," I tell her. "I've come to visit, if that's okay? But say if you don't feel like company. I won't mind."

"How lovely!" Mrs. G. smiles, her wrinkles briefly ironed out with pleasure. "Come on in, dear. Do you mind taking your shoes off?"

Even though we've lived next door to Mrs. Gayatri for ten years, I've never once stepped inside this house, and it feels strange following Mrs. G. into the hallway. I take my shoes off and put them on the mat.

"I don't get many visitors," she says, sighing as she leads me into a rather dark living room. She points to the red velvet armchair. "Sit yourself down. Can I get you a tea or coffee? Will you help me eat this cake?"

While she makes the tea, I sit looking around the room. There's a slight smell of incense and a small statue in the corner that is part elephant, part man. There are photos—some very old sepia ones of people that look like they were taken in India. There's one black-and-white wedding photo, and I wonder if it's Mrs. Gayatri's own wedding picture. I go closer to look.

Mrs. G. comes back in with flowery teacups and saucers on a tray. She sets the tray down on a small, dark, wooden table and then goes back for the cake slices on two matching china plates.

"I was just looking at your pictures. I hope you don't mind," I say.

"That was my wedding—so, so many years ago." She smiles. "My darling husband Vijay. He died ten years ago, and I still miss him so much. These are my parents—they of course died many, many years ago—and my five big brothers, too."

"Do you have no other family—no children of your own?" I ask.

Mrs. G.'s mouth turns down. Her eyes look suddenly glassy, and I wish I hadn't asked.

"I'm so sorry—I didn't mean to upset you," I say.

"It's fine," she assures me. "Just hard when everyone I love has gone." She sighs again. "Life must be hard for you, too, being stuck at home so much."

"At least I have my mom," I say. "She's had to give up her job to look after me, though. And Dad's working harder than ever."

"Are you not going to school at all?"

"Not since last June," I explain. "I have a tutor who comes once a week. I have constant pain in my arms and legs, and I just get so tired when I do anything. It's really frustrating. But I think I am improving now."

"What is the cause?" she asks. "Do they know why it started?"

I shake my head. "I had tonsillitis, and I just didn't get better. No one knows why it happens."

"And is there treatment for it?"

"There's some research going on, but they know so little about it, there isn't much to offer. I'm on a waiting list to see a consultant. The doctor just told me to try to pace myself."

"But you will recover?"

"I hope so."

There's silence for a moment. I don't want to think about my illness—about the possibility that I'll be like this forever. I change the subject.

"Mrs. Gayatri, I wanted to ask you something," I say now. "I'm interested in the history of our street, and I know you've lived here a long time. I wondered if you have any memories to share of anything that has happened here?"

"What kind of thing?" she asks.

"Any memorable events, things that shocked you, tragedies?"

"That's a strange question!" Mrs. G. shakes her head. "It would be better to focus your energies on happier things. Let me think... Now there's Amir and Zainab, of course, across the street. Their daughter died. That was most certainly a tragedy. She was so young. Their only child. That must have been twenty-five years ago. But that's probably not the sort of thing you mean. Now, what else..."

"The girl across the street—can you tell me more?" I ask, leaning forward. "What happened to her?"

Mrs. G. shakes her head. "Really, it is upsetting for me

even to think about it. Let's talk about happier things and leave the past behind. It will do your health no good to focus on such sadness. Should I show you what came in that package the other day?"

I nod. I'm frustrated. I am desperate to know more but I don't want to push her if it's upsetting her. She walks slowly back into the kitchen and returns with a bird feeder.

"I love my garden, but I'm not up to tending it like I used to," she tells me. "I like to watch the birds, though. I wondered, since you're here, whether you might do me a favor and hang it outside for me—on the silver birch. I have the seeds to fill it with. Then I can sit by the back window and watch for the birds. They'll be grateful now the weather's getting colder." This sounds sad to me—having nothing more interesting to do than watching birds, though maybe it is no sadder than watching the street like I do. I nod again and follow her to the back door, which she unlocks. The garden, which looked overgrown when I last glimpsed it from my parents' bedroom window, looks far wilder from down here. Neglect has turned it into a jungle.

"This garden was beautiful once," Mrs. G. says wistfully. "My husband and I—we were both gardeners. But now I don't have the strength for it, nor the money to pay someone."

"I wish I could help," I tell her, "but I don't have the strength, either."

Actually, it's the last thing I'd want to do, even if I did have full strength. Gardening isn't my idea of fun at all.

"Of course you don't, my dear, but it's a kind thought."

She seems so sad as I struggle for something positive to say. "I guess it's good for wildlife?"

"True," she says, but I sense this is little consolation. I fill the feeder and find I can easily hang it on a branch. Mrs. G.'s house is on the corner, and it's the only one in our row that has a decent-sized yard. I've never been very interested in gardens, but I do vaguely remember it being much neater in the past. I used to be jealous as a young child, because we only have a small cement back patio with no lawn or plants at all.

"Thank you so much!" she says. "That's wonderful. I'd have to stand on a stool to do that, and I knew it wasn't a good idea."

"No, you shouldn't go doing things like that," I agree. "It's nice to be able to do something helpful for a change. It's usually me who needs the help."

"Well, I'm very grateful," she says.

"I'd better go now," I tell her. I suddenly feel so tired—and she is looking tired, too. She doesn't protest, and I wonder if I have already outstayed my welcome.

"I hope you will come again," she says. "It's been so nice to have some company."

I'm relieved. I was worried I'd upset her asking about tragedies, and that she wouldn't want me back. I'm glad I came, though—Mrs. G. did seem genuinely happy to see me, and I even learned something about the girl across the street. At least, I may have done. I learned there was a tragedy, and it involved a girl who died. Does that mean the girl I see really is a ghost? I wish I knew the whole story.

"A gummy bear factory! My son is making gummy bears?"

Dad has somehow seen Mom's latest message from Marek, who has moved from sprinkling cheese on pizzas to making gummy bears. Dad is reeling off a torrent of Polish insults.

"Why my son? Why me? We bring him here for a good life, he has a good education, and he throws it all away to make teddy bear sweets! What did I do to deserve this useless child?"

"Don't say that, Dad," I protest. Dad has a tendency to be overly dramatic, but to me this seems unfair.

"Sorry, *moje kochanie*, I don't want to upset you." Dad gently strokes my hair. "But gummy bears! *Pah!*"

A few days later I get a package from Germany. Marek has written a card saying how much he misses me and enclosed five packets of gummy bears. I wish he'd come home.

I have a bad day for no apparent reason. That's what it's like. I spend the morning in bed eating gummy bears and then the afternoon sitting up, looking out of the window. I've been looking out every day, but I haven't seen the girl again.

Mom is worrying that I'm seeing things—as in imagining them. I overheard her telling Dad. I get brain fog sometimes. I can't think straight and I struggle with the schoolwork my tutor leaves for me, but hallucinations are not a symptom of ME. I know that because I looked it up online. Even so, the more I watch from the window and don't see the girl, the more I doubt my own memory. I'm wondering if I really saw her at all or if it was a trick of the light. It's easier to think of her as a ghost than as a real person—but if she was real, maybe she was staying there and now she's gone. I hope so, but either way, I can't stop thinking about her. I wish I could.

It's almost a relief when my home tutor, Judy, gets here and I can think of something else. She sits on the wicker chair in my room, runs her hand through her thick dark hair, and adjusts her big glasses as she checks my attempts at some math problems. I'm panicking that I'm getting so far behind at school.

"I want you to give me more work, Judy," I tell her. "I'm not doing enough. How am I ever going to catch up?"

"You can only do what you can do," she says. "I don't want to give you too much. It will stress you out, and that'll set you back further. But you're doing okay, and you *are* getting better. You couldn't have done math like this a few weeks ago."

"My head is less fuzzy," I agree, "but, Judy, I'm so far behind! Even if I get back to school, how will I get caught up?"

"Maybe you could cut down on the number of classes?" she suggests.

I shake my head. "I don't want to give any up."

"Or you could perhaps stay in tenth grade, repeat the year."

"Never," I say emphatically. "Can you imagine how awful that would be? I want to be with my friends."

"Don't think about it now," Judy tells me. "Keep working like you are and get plenty of rest, too. Just focus on one day at a time."

It's easy for her to say, but the thought of repeating tenth grade, while my friends move on without me, is more than I can take. I won't let that happen. I have to get better and back to school as soon as possible. If Judy won't give me more work, then I will get it from Ellie.

Once Judy's gone, I work hard on more math, but I'm exhausted, and I don't manage as much as I'd hoped. My eyes are drooping. I wish I had more energy and could concentrate better. But Judy has said that I'm improving. So that gives me hope.

The next day, Ellie is due to visit, and this time I'm determined to remember to tell her about the girl, since I'm positive she'll be able to help me think it through. But when she arrives she's with Lia, and I'm not sure how I feel about it. Lia's in our grade, but I don't know her that well. We've never been friends.

"You were moaning that no one else comes to see you, so I brought Lia," Ellie tells me. "We've been working together in drama. We've done this sketch—you really should see it. It's hilarious! We might even do it in the show next semester!"

She exchanges glances with Lia, and they both start giggling. They're clearly waiting for me to ask them to perform it for me. I feel a tingle of jealousy that they seem so close. I wonder if Lia's trying to replace me as Ellie's bestie—but I am also curious about this sketch.

"You going to show me then?" I ask.

"Okay—with any luck a laugh will do you good and not tire you out," Ellie says, grinning.

The sketch has me in stitches—I laugh so much that I ache. It may hurt physically, but I do feel better inside.

"Do you think you'll be back at school soon?" Lia asks, when we can finally speak again.

I shrug. "I hope so."

"You must be so bored stuck in here," she says. "Or have you been doing some writing? That story you wrote was so terrific—it's fantastic that you've won that competition!"

She sounds genuinely happy for me, and my feelings toward her soften.

"I don't really feel up to writing," I tell her. "I'm sure I will get back to it soon, though."

"Lia and I are going to Dimitri's New Year's Eve party!" Ellie says.

"Dimitri's? But you can't stand him!"

"Oh—he's all right. Lots of people are going."

"Could be fun, I guess."

"Yeah, well, I'll tell you how it goes," Ellie says, laughing.

"Who throws up where and when, you mean?" Lia giggles.

Ellie turns to me. "Remember that time at Erin's party, Kas?" She grins. "When you had to rescue me?"

"What happened?" asks Lia.

It takes a few seconds, but eventually the memory comes flooding back. "Oh, yeah! You got locked in the bathroom!" I laugh.

"There was someone in the downstairs bathroom, so I had to go upstairs," Ellie tells Lia. "Then the door wouldn't open and I was yelling and yelling—but the music was so loud no one heard me."

"And I was dancing with Serene and Erin," I say, "and waiting for you, and you took forever, so in the end I came up to look for you and heard you shouting!"

"So how did you get out?" Lia asks.

"Erin found a screwdriver and unlocked the door handle," I tell her.

"I'd have been stuck there for hours otherwise," says Ellie. "I thought I was going to have to climb out the tiny bathroom window and shinny down the drainpipe!"

Now it's me and Ellie laughing together, and Lia's turn to join in.

After they leave, I feel glad that Lia came. Ellie will always be my best friend, but it was nice to talk to someone else for a change.

I turn my chair back to the window and sit looking out. It's weird, thinking back to Erin's party dancing and laughing with my friends, having fun. It's like that was another lifetime. But I will get better. I am determined to get back to those things. I see movement in the corner of my eye, but when I look there's nothing. Did the curtain move? Was she there, and did she fade away instantly, as always? I wanted to wave—to let her know I'm here. Maybe she'd stay visible if she knew someone could see her.

I need to find out more. I don't want to upset Mrs. G., but right now she's the only one who can help. I need to talk to her again.

I've knocked on the door, and I'm waiting and waiting for Mrs. Gayatri to come and answer it.

She looks surprised. "How are you, dear?" she asks. "What can I do for you?"

"I thought I'd come for a chat, but only if it's convenient," I say.

She smiles and holds the door for me.

"I'm so glad you came again," she says. "Those hungry birds have gone through all the food already. I've seen starlings there, and robins. If you could refill the bird feeder for me, I'd be so pleased."

"Of course," I tell her.

"You do that while I make some tea."

When I've refilled the feeder, we sit on armchairs opposite each other.

"Mrs. Gayatri, you know you told me about the girl who died across the street? I don't want to upset you, but I'd really like to know more about what happened."

She frowns. "To lose your only child—it's such a sad thing," she says quietly. "She was a sweet girl. Meningitis, it was. There's nothing more to tell really."

"Meningitis?" I repeat. "So, she was sick?"

I was expecting something more dramatic—something that would give a reason for her to be appearing as a ghost.

Mrs. G. nods. "Nasty illness that—can still be a killer, even now. Her parents moved away in the end. I think it was hard for them to see..." She pauses, her eyes glassy for a moment. "To see other children growing up on the street when their child was no longer there. It was empty for over a year after they moved, number forty-six. I think people viewing the house could still sense the sadness."

"You mean forty-eight?" I ask.

"Forty-eight? No." Mrs. G. frowns. "What makes you say that? It was forty-six."

"Forty-six?" I stare at her in surprise. "Are you sure?"

"Yes." She nods firmly. "Poor Shari, she was only five, you know."

I am speechless, silent, as I try to take this in. This isn't about my girl at all—it's the wrong house, and the girl is the wrong age. So now I'm back to knowing nothing at all!

Mrs. G. looks so sad. I know it was a tragic thing, but I'm surprised that she is this upset.

"I'm so sorry I asked you about it," I tell her. "I didn't mean to upset you."

"Never mind," she says. "Let's say no more about it."

It's Christmas Eve. We were supposed to be in Poland having a big family celebration, like last year. My cousin Aleksandra and I had such a great time together, walking around the Christmas markets, so pretty in the crisp, white snow, and then back to my aunt and uncle's for delicious hot chocolate. Christmas in Lodz is like the pictures you get in England on Christmas cards, but I've never actually seen snow in England at Christmas. I like living here, but I love spending Christmas in Poland, and I especially love the buzz of being part of a much larger family—that's something I never feel here in England.

But we're not there because I'm not strong enough for the long journey, and I feel so bad about it. Mom is trying to put on a brave face. Dad is taking a chance to do some DIY—fixing a cupboard door that never shuts and putting up a new shelf in the kitchen. The banging is giving me a headache, and I'm relieved when it stops.

Then it's too quiet—especially without Marek.

I've been hoping desperately that he might come home for Christmas, that he'll just turn up and surprise us. We've never had a Christmas without the four of us being together. He hasn't been in touch. Even as the fish is cooking for our traditional Christmas Eve meal, there's a sound outside, and Mom rushes to the front door, but it was only someone leaving a flyer.

We eat our Christmas Eve meal—twelve different dishes including fried fish and potatoes—and Mom goes to church for midnight Mass and then again on Christmas morning. Dad stays with me. He's never been too interested in church. He finds YouTube clips of funny kittens attacking Christmas trees to show me, trying to cheer us both up.

"I'm so sorry, Dad," I tell him.

"What you have to be sorry for?" he asks gently.

"I know you love Christmas in Poland with Uncle Andrzej and Auntie Maria as much as Mom does. It's all my fault."

"My lovely girl, we'll soon have you well. We will be in Poland again—maybe in the summer."

"I hope so, Dad."

Mom is trying so hard. She's made her special Christmas cake. We have an amazing tree. But where's Marek? We still haven't heard from him. He hasn't even responded to my messages.

The radio and TV give the impression of fun, but there are

no cousins chattering and laughing, no aunt and uncle bickering, which makes me think of Mrs. Gayatri. It must be like this for her all the time.

"I'm feeling bad that Mrs. Gayatri is on her own," I say to Mom. "Maybe we could ask her over for Christmas dinner later?"

We had our main meal last night, but we like to adopt some English traditions, too, and are having turkey for Christmas day.

Mom hesitates. "I'm not sure, love. She's a Hindu. I don't think she'll want to celebrate Christmas."

"But she's all alone," I say, frowning.

Mom meets my eyes, smiling softly. "There's no harm in asking her, if you want to."

I go next door, knock and wait.

"Happy Christmas!" Mrs. G. says as she opens it. "I didn't expect to see you today. Aren't you busy celebrating?"

"We usually go to Poland," I tell her, "but I'm not well enough to travel. We wondered if you'd like to join us for dinner. Unless it's against your religion?"

"How kind! I don't celebrate Christmas, but I would be glad of company today—if you're sure. Oh, but I am vegetarian. Is that a problem? I could always eat before I come..."

"It won't be a problem," I say, hoping that's true.

"That is very kind—please tell your parents not to go to any trouble. What time would you like me?"

"Three p.m."

"I will see you then." Mrs. G. smiles warmly. "Thank you for thinking of me, Kasia."

I feel good as I go back home and tell Mom that Mrs. G. has said yes. "Mom, she seemed really happy to be asked."

"Well, there's plenty of food!" Mom smiles.

"Actually, she's vegetarian," I announce.

"Oh." Mom frowns. "What should I do? She can't just eat potatoes and Brussels sprouts!"

I shrug. "I'm sure she doesn't mind what she eats, as long as it isn't meat. She was just happy to be invited."

"Maybe if I add something spicy," says Mom, tutting. She opens the cupboard where she keeps herbs and spices and starts rummaging. "I don't have many spices, but I'll see what I can do. Oh, Kasia—I feel awful. I know you're trying to be kind, but it will be so embarrassing."

"Please don't worry, Mom," I tell her, and now I feel guilty for stressing her out when I'm not even up to helping with the cooking.

Dad makes a face when I say Mrs. G. is coming. "I was going to have a nice nap in front of the TV. Now I'll have to dress up?" he asks.

"Not dress up—just dress, Dad," I tell him. He's still in his pajamas.

It's his turn to pout. "And what will we talk about? We have nothing in common."

I'm beginning to feel a little stressed myself now, so I go and lie down on the sofa. To my surprise I go to sleep and when I wake up, Mom is poking something in my face.

"Here, Kasia—taste this," Mom says, holding out a spoon of brownish mush. "It's a curried lentil dish. I didn't have all of the ingredients, so I don't know if it's all right or not."

I taste the food, and I'm about to tell her it's fine when suddenly it feels like my mouth is on fire! I rush for a glass of water, but it's a long time before I can speak.

"Oh, Mom! How much chili did you put in that?" I ask, my eyes watering.

"I'm not sure," she says. "So—no good then?" She takes a taste, too.

We look at each other—and then suddenly we're both laughing. Mom's usually so good at cooking, but this is really terrible.

Dad comes and looks at us, laughing and crying together, and backs off hastily, muttering in Polish.

"Oh dear," Mom says when she can talk again. "I'm running out of time. I'll make a salad, too—that will have to do."

When Mrs. G. arrives, she brings a large plastic bowl with a lid. "I couldn't expect you to cook specially for me," she says, "so I've made a dish with chickpeas and vegetables that we can all share."

"It smells wonderful," says Mom, smiling.

Mrs. G.'s dish is full of flavor, but it isn't spicy-hot at all. Even Dad tries some of it and declares it delicious. "Complements the turkey perfectly," he tells Mrs. G., who beams back at him, delighted.

We talk about the snowy Christmases in Poland, and Mrs. G. tells us about her first experience of snow when she came to this country in 1974. Mom then tells her about when we moved to the UK.

"We came in 2005—the economy was so bad in Poland. Stefan realized that he could earn as much here in one week, no—one day, as he could earn in a month in Lodz."

"That's why you came?" Mrs. G. asks.

"Yes—we thought we were coming to paradise, you know? We found an amazing house on the internet, and the price looked so good. It was near Manor House and Seven Sisters. Then we arrived and discovered we were paying for one room only. There were twenty other people sharing the house! It was such a shock. Later, we met kinder people, though—people who helped us."

Mom and Dad ask Mrs. G. about her life and family, but she gives short answers and quickly turns the conversation back to us. Dad starts telling us jokes, and some even make Mrs. G. laugh out loud. She surprises us by telling a few good ones herself. Then Dad does his party trick of making his ears waggle. His face goes bright red when he does it, and his eyes look like they're popping out.

"Well, in all my years, I have never met anyone who can do that!" Mrs. G. chuckles. "I am having the loveliest time. Thank you so much."

"And now please join us in our special after-dinner ceremony!" Dad announces.

Mrs. G. looks slightly worried.

"What ceremony?" I demand.

"The 'let's sit in the family room and watch TV' ceremony," Dad says, waving his arms in a triumphant gesture.

Mrs. G. smiles with relief.

"Are you up to watching a little, my *kotku*?" Dad asks me.

I've been having a good day, but now I realize I need a rest. The glands in my neck have started throbbing, and my legs feel achy. I can't cope with watching TV, but I lie on the sofa with my eyes shut while the others all watch a movie. I am so happy we invited Mrs. G.—they are all getting along so well.

Afterward we play charades. I'm not up to performing but guess some of the answers. I laugh so hard at Dad's James Bond impression that my throat hurts. I'm feeling happy, though, when I excuse myself and go upstairs to bed.

9

I'm sitting in the kitchen with Mom, eating freshly baked orange and almond cake. It's one of my grandmother's recipes that Mom is trying to re-create from memory. She's always wishing she had the old family recipe book, but that got left behind in Poland. I'm lucky that I don't gain weight easily, even though I'm not exercising much—but still, I am trying not to eat too much cake.

"It's not like my mother's. What do you think, Kasia?"

"It's so good!" I moan.

"It's a big one—I'll have to freeze most of it," Mom tells me.

"Can I take some to Mrs. Gayatri?" I ask.

"What a nice idea," says Mom. "I think she enjoyed Christmas with us, didn't she?"

She cuts a large slice of cake and wraps it in foil, while I put my coat on. It's the middle of January and getting colder every day and dark so early, too. I knock on the door. I wait, knowing that as usual she may take some time. Maybe it's just the cold, but I feel as if I've been waiting longer than usual. I knock again. There's still no answer. Maybe Mrs. G. is out on one of her rare trips to the stores. I turn to go back home but something stops me. What if she is there, but she's sick or something? I knock harder. Then I lift the mail slot flap and call through.

"Mrs. Gayatri! It's Kasia."

No answer. I try to look through the mail slot in the door. It isn't easy to see through, but I'm sure there's a dark shape on the floor at the end of the hallway by the kitchen.

"Mrs. Gayatri! It's Kasia. Are you okay?"

As my eyes adjust to the gloom, I make out a shoe shape. A shoe and part of a leg. I gasp. It's her! She's lying there on the floor, not moving...not moving at all.

I try the side gate, but it's locked, so I come back to the front. I put the cake down on the doorstep and keep calling her through the mail slot, at the same time reaching into my coat pocket for my phone. My hand is shaking, and I can hardly get a grip on it. I call 911.

"Ambulance please!" My voice comes out squeaky, not like my normal voice at all. "It's my neighbor. She's lying on the floor in her hallway, and she's not moving. I can see her through her mail slot. It's forty-seven New Weald Road."

They ask me questions that I wish I could answer with "yes." Can I get in? Do I know where she keeps a spare key? Do I have a phone number for a family member?

I check under the doormat and in the flowerpots by the front door, but I can't find a key. There's a small, inauspicious pile of rocks on the other side of the door, and half-heartedly I lift those, too, and reveal two keys. I look down the road, hoping the ambulance will appear and I'll be able to hand the keys over without going in myself. Should I call Mom? No, I have to go in. I fiddle with the keys, my hands still shaking, and the door clicks open.

I hesitate—scared, scared to go closer. Maybe Mrs. G. is dead. I don't want to see her close up if she is. I can imagine her eyes—glassy and scary like in the movies. If she *is* dead, should I close them? I've seen that in movies, too, but I don't want to touch a dead person.

Mrs. Gayatri is lying crumpled, her feet sticking out at an awkward angle through the doorway to the kitchen. I can't see her head. I edge nearer, on tiptoes for some reason, as if any sound might wake her—but I want her to wake up. I want it more than anything.

"Mrs. Gayatri?" I call.

I bend over her. She seems to jerk slightly. Her head is on one side. There's blood, a gash on the side of her head and a pool of blood underneath. I gulp. Nausea rises in my throat. It looks as if someone has hit her hard on the head. Did someone attack her? Something is sparkling on the floor beside her. Fragments of glass. Did someone hit her over the head with a bottle or a vase? Then I see a dark wooden photo frame on the floor. Someone must have hit her and she fell against the wall, knocking the picture off its hook.

My heart is pounding. Taking care not to step on the glass, I crouch and put my hand under Mrs. G.'s nose. To my relief I feel air moving. She is definitely breathing.

"Mrs. Gayatri! Mrs. Gayatri!" I call. "It's Kasia from next door. Don't worry—an ambulance is coming."

A small sound comes from her, but it isn't words. I wait. It feels like forever. I feel so alone, with such a huge responsibility—someone's life and there's nothing I can do except crouch here and hold her hand.

I wonder what Mom would do, and then I call her. She says she'll come right away. I've got this weird, floaty feeling in my stomach, like the inside of a lava lamp. I glance down at the frame. The picture, which I think is of Mrs. G.'s husband when he was young, has slipped out, and there is another photo behind it. I see it is a picture of Mr. and Mrs. G. with a girl around my age standing between them, smiling straight into the camera.

Before I have time to wonder about this girl, Mom arrives and has her arms around my shoulder, and the ambulance is here, too, with two paramedics.

"You're her neighbor? Maybe you can give us a few details," one of the paramedics asks Mom. "What is her full name, date of birth? Do you know her next of kin?"

Mom can only give Mrs. G.'s last name. She never told us

her first name or her birthday, and she has no family that we knew of.

The paramedic turns to me. "Kasia, is it? You're the one who called us? You did the right thing."

"You should call the police," I tell her. "I think she was attacked—see that gash on her head?"

"You saw someone attack her?" she asks, looking alarmed.

"No, no." I shake my head. This is so awful.

"Looks like a stroke to me," I hear her say. "She must have hit her head on the wall as she fell. That's why it's bleeding. There's no sign of an attack, is there?" she asks the other paramedic who is examining Mrs. G.

"No," comes the answer.

"But...the gash..." I say. "I thought...the blood..." I can feel my cheeks flushing red with embarrassment.

"She has a big imagination," I hear Mom say quietly, embarrassing me even more.

"Mom..."

"You did a good thing," Mom says to me now, squeezing my shoulders. "My Kasia, you're a good, brave girl."

As Mrs. Gayatri is carried out on a stretcher, I realize I still have the photo in my hand. Who is the girl standing in the middle, and why was this picture hidden behind another? I stare at it for a moment, then tuck the photo under my coat.

I turn toward the ambulance. "Do you think she'll be okay?" I ask the paramedic.

"She's in the best hands now," she replies.

The doors slam and the ambulance disappears down the road.

Mom squeezes my hand. "So sad," she says, "to see her like that."

"You don't think she's going to die, do you?" I ask.

"I hope not," says Mom. "I offered to go with her in the ambulance, but they said no."

"I think I need to lie down," I tell her, as exhaustion suddenly overtakes me.

"I'm not surprised—what a shocking thing!" says Mom. "Thank goodness you found her, that's all I can say, or who knows how much longer she could have been lying there. I'll call the hospital later, and maybe go and visit her tomorrow."

When Dad comes home, we tell him all about it. "I do feel sorry for the woman, not having family around her," says Dad. "But try not to get too involved, okay?" He gives Mom a hug.

Later, I lay in bed looking at the photo. Mrs. G. looks much younger, but the girl couldn't be her daughter, could she? Mrs. G. would have mentioned her when I asked if she had any children. I think back, trying to remember her exact words. "*It's sad when everyone you love has gone.*" It was something like that.

The way the girl is standing between Mr. and Mrs. Gayatri—it definitely looks like a daughter with her parents. Unless she was a visitor—a niece or something. Maybe

Mrs. G. did have a daughter and she died—like the girl at number 46. But then why would she cover her photo? I'm sure she'd want to remember her.

I put the photo in my bottom drawer with the daffodil card that Josh signed, planning to give it back when Mrs. G. is home.

Mom calls the hospital to find out how Mrs. G. is, but since she's not family they are reluctant to tell her anything. Eventually they tell her that Mrs. G. definitely had a stroke but that she's doing okay.

The next day Mom says she's going to visit her. I wish I could go, too, but I am not well enough. I feel wiped out.

"Mom, before you go, take a look at this," I say. I get the photo out of the drawer and tell her how I found it behind the picture in the smashed frame.

"Why did you take it?" Mom asks, frowning as she looks at it closely. "You should have left it where you found it."

"Mom—don't you think it looks like Mrs. G. had a daughter? The way she's standing between them?"

"Maybe," says Mom, nodding.

"Why would she hide the picture away and say she has no family?" I ask.

"I don't know, Kasia, I really don't."

"Maybe you should take the picture with you to the hospital," I tell her. "They wanted to know her next of kin, didn't they? Maybe show them."

"Yes," says Mom, though she looks a little hesitant. "I don't want to interfere, but I guess it doesn't do any harm to take it."

When Mom's gone, I struggle out of bed and sit by the window. I look at the house across from mine and I think about the face I saw—the girl. I wish she'd appear now, but she doesn't.

I'm lying down again when Mom comes back. I hear her feet hurrying up the stairs, faster than usual for Mom.

"Is Mrs. G. okay?" I ask, suddenly worried.

"Yes, she's improving," Mom says, sitting on the edge of my bed. "She's able to talk, though her words are a little slurred. She was really glad to see me. The nurses were happy she had a visitor, too, since no one else has been to see her, and they said there's no next of kin to call on. So, then I got out the photo."

"Really? What happened?" I ask eagerly. I pull myself into a partial sitting position and Mom plumps up my pillow.

"We showed her the photo," Mom tells me. "I felt very awkward—I thought Mrs. G. was going to get angry, but she had tears in her eyes. She admitted that the girl is her daughter. Can you believe it?"

"Why has she kept her secret?" I ask. "Why did she hide the photo?"

"Apparently they haven't spoken for eighteen years," says Mom. "Mrs. G. said she has no idea where she is now."

"So, they might not be able to find her?" I ask.

"They're going to try," Mom tells me. "Mrs. G. gave them her daughter's full name and date of birth, so we'll have to wait and see. If they find her, I only hope the daughter wants to see her mom. It's going to be very upsetting for Mrs. G. if not."

"It's so sad that they had a falling-out," I say. "Did she say why?"

"No," Mom tells me.

"You should have asked," I say.

"It's none of our business, Kasia," says Mom. "She'll tell us if she wants us to know."

I know what Mom's saying, but I'm frustrated. For a mother and daughter not to speak for eighteen years, it must have been something big.

Later I get up again and sit at the window looking out. There's no sign of the girl across the street. There's an old woman at the bus stop. Her shopping bag is bulging, and she leans it against the bench. She's looking at the timetable now, but the bag is unbalanced, and, as I'm watching, it tips. A lemon falls out, followed by a box of crackers.

There's a boy walking past, and he sees what's happened and stops. I gasp a little when I realize it's Josh. I haven't seen him for so long—he looks taller, and his hair is longer. He crouches down and helps to gather the things. What a nice thing to do. The woman thanks him profusely. I've seen her there before, and it's clear from her expression that she doesn't have time for teenagers, thinking they are trouble with their rowdy music and phones, so Josh has taken her by surprise with his kindness. The old woman sits on the bench and tries once more to balance the bag, this time against one leg as she sits, with the other leg supporting it, too. Hopefully it won't fall now. She watches Josh walk away—and so do I, longingly.

I wish I could call him. I wish he'd look up at the window and see me, but he doesn't. I watch him walk away until I can't see him anymore.

10

I'm sitting at the kitchen table, drinking an herbal tea mix called "Energy" while Mom's cooking chicken soup. This January weather is still so cold and gloomy, we need it to warm us up. Steam rises from the stove. "It's only two weeks until the award ceremony," I remind Mom. "I'm so excited about it."

"Yes—I want to talk to you about that," Mom says.

I look up to meet her eyes. Her serious expression makes me anxious.

"Is it Dad—can't he come?" I ask.

"He won't know until the last minute, Kasia. It isn't that."

"What, then?"

Mom sighs as she breaks noodles into the soup. "I'm so glad you're doing much better—coming downstairs, going next door," she says, "but it will be a long day, and I'm worried it'll be too exhausting for you."

I look at her in horror. "I have to go, Mom. I just have to! It's the only thing I've been looking forward to."

"I do want you to go," Mom tells me. "I just don't want you to undo all the progress you've made. There's so much to think about—there might be a lot of standing, and we might not be able stop the car near the theater, so there will be walking, too."

"But Mom!" I glare at her fiercely.

"Let me finish, Kasia." Mom holds up a hand to stop me. "I've been making calls, and I've found out we can get a wheelchair on loan. What do you think about that?"

"A wheelchair?"

This isn't what I was expecting. I feel all mixed up: relief that this isn't a fight about not going, but also sadness and bitterness. Also, am I really so sick that I need a wheelchair? It feels like a backward step.

"It will be less tiring for you," Mom says.

"I hope you're not saying I should start using one all the time?" I ask.

"No, of course not. Just for this one occasion—and maybe other times to do things that would otherwise be too much. Let's just try it—that's all I'm saying."

The idea of not having to walk, not having to stand, definitely makes the whole outing feel more doable. "Okay," I tell her. "Just this once."

When the wheelchair arrives, Mom wants me to sit in it and try it right away.

"I will be a learner driver, I need to practice!" she says.

I wish I could push myself, but my arms aren't strong enough, and this wheelchair is the kind with small wheels that's made to be pushed.

"I don't feel like it right now," I say, though, really, I don't want to see the looks I'll get from people we pass on the street—pitying looks.

"We need to try it sometime," says Mom—but she doesn't mention it again until a few days later, when she says, "Do you feel up to coming with me to visit Mrs. Gayatri? I'm sure she'd be pleased to see you." Then she adds tentatively, "I thought it would be a chance to try out the wheelchair."

I am still not happy about the wheelchair idea, but I'd rather try it out in a hospital than along our street, and I would like to visit Mrs. G.

"Just make sure you can push it without tipping me out facedown," I tease Mom. "Although, at least there'd be doctors on hand if that happened!"

She laughs.

I haven't been in a car for months. The seat belt is uncomfortable, and I feel giddy as the car pulls away. I look out of the window and try to pretend I'm okay.

When we reach the hospital, Mom struggles to lift the wheelchair out of the car and get it open. I wait patiently in the passenger seat, wishing I could help. At last, I'm in the chair, and she wheels me up the ramp into the building and down a series of long corridors. Mom's having no trouble pushing me and no one gives us a second glance. It feels strange but okay and I am relieved not to have to walk all this way.

Mrs. Gayatri smiles a slightly lopsided but clearly happy smile as we arrive.

"Good idea," she comments, "using a wheelchair until you get your strength back. It's so nice of you to come and see me. And your mother was telling me you have your writing award ceremony soon!" she says. "I will look forward to hearing all about it."

I nod. "I can't wait!"

Mom pulls up a chair, and I stand up and go sit on it while she parks the wheelchair in the corner.

"How are you?" I ask Mrs. G. "Are you going home soon?"

"In two or three days' time, they tell me," she says. "And I have some wonderful news!"

"Your daughter?" I ask, eagerly. "Have they found her?"

"Yes! Oh, Kasia, I didn't think she would want to see me. She hasn't been in touch in all these years. But they contacted her, and she is coming! I wish it hadn't taken something like this, but still, I cannot wait to see her—and I have a grandson, too! They are coming to visit tomorrow."

"Wow!" I say.

She reaches out a hand and I offer mine, which she squeezes gently. "And it is thanks to you," she says more quietly. "It is thanks to you that I am alive and also that I will see Devi again, and meet my grandson. That photo... I couldn't understand where it had come from, but your mother explained about the broken frame."

"Can I ask..." I begin, eager to know more, but I see Mom shaking her head sternly and I stop.

"Ask what, my dear?" says Mrs. G.

"Oh...just...er... How are you going to manage back at home on your own?"

"The staff at the hospital have told me they will send in people to help me every day. Oh, I will be so glad to be back in my own home."

"And I'll come in to visit more often," I tell her.

"That will be lovely," she says, nodding.

"And if you need anything, you must ask us," adds Mom.

11

Next time Ellie comes to visit, she brings Lia again. They are sitting cross-legged next to each other on my bed, while I sit on the wicker chair.

"I've brought you some homework, like you asked," Ellie says, handing me a pile of papers. "But I have no idea why you want this stuff when you don't have to do it."

"I've got to do it, or I'll never catch up," I tell her.

"Well, if there's anything you don't understand, just ask me," says Ellie. "But don't knock yourself out trying to do too much."

"You sound like my mom—and Judy," I say, smiling. Ellie shrugs. "I just want you to get better, so you can get back to school—oh—and so you can come to parties like Dimitri's and Tilly's party last week, too!"

"How was it?" I ask.

"Actually, it wasn't that great," says Ellie.

"What happened?" I ask. "Anyone there you liked?"

"It's all about pairing off with someone," she moans. "That's all anyone seems to care about—and if you're not interested, they just think you're playing hard to get. I had two boys almost fighting over me at one point, when I'd already told them both to get lost. Erin ended up with Kai, though."

"How about you?" I ask Lia. She blushes and just shakes her head.

"So, it wasn't much fun?" I ask.

Lia and Ellie exchange a quick glance as if sharing a private joke. I feel left out—they are becoming best friends I can see it.

"Dimitri's party was better," says Lia, turning back to me. "He was so funny—he was acting totally wasted, like he could hardly stand up, but it turned out he was only pretending, and he hadn't had a drop."

"Why would he do that?" I laugh.

"I think he wanted to stay sober to make sure no one wrecked his parents' place." She laughs, too, and Ellie joins in.

They don't seem to have anything else to tell me, so I tell them about Mrs. G.'s stroke.

"You probably saved her life," Lia says, clearly impressed. "It must have been so scary. It makes me think I should do a first aid class."

"I went to see her in the hospital," I tell them.

"And you managed that okay?" says Ellie. "Does that

mean you're well enough to go the awards ceremony? It's next week, isn't it?"

I nod. "I hope so. Mom's rented a wheelchair for me."

They both look a little shocked at this, and I wish I hadn't said it.

"Miss Giles is coming, too."

"Really? That's nice. Did you know that she's helping with the end-of-term show? She's been great," Ellie says. "Look, I'm sorry I haven't seen you more. We're rehearsing, and my mom's stressing out, because she thinks I should be spending more time studying. She didn't want me to do the show in the first place, but I convinced her I could do it and study. Now I'm not so sure. I didn't realize there would be quite so many rehearsals. Lia is so good in it! I hope you can come and see it, Kasia."

"I'll see how I do at the awards," I tell her. "If I manage that okay, maybe I can come to the show."

"I'll keep my fingers crossed," says Ellie. "I'd love for you to be there."

Last year I was there—not in the audience but in the orchestra for the first time. Our school has really good music and drama departments, and they put on a show every Easter. Although I was nervous, it was amazing being part of it. I was looking forward to doing it again this year, but now I will be lucky if I am well enough to watch.

Dad still doesn't know if he'll be able to get time off for

the award ceremony, but Miss Giles has offered to take us since Mom is worried about driving in central London. I am so excited, but also scared that I won't feel well enough on the day. I stay upstairs for a few days before the event, hoping to conserve my energy, but I can't help being anxious, and I know that makes me worse.

On the day, I am relieved to find I don't feel too bad. Miss Giles also seems really excited when she comes to pick us up.

"I've entered students before for this award," she tells me, "but I've never had anyone win! They get thousands of entries from all over the country, you know. Most people will have traveled much farther than us. There are categories for different age-groups and genres, so with family members included, I think there will be over a hundred people there."

When we arrive, Miss Giles drops us off as near to the theater as she can and goes to park the car. She says she'll catch up with us inside. Mom pushes me the rest of the way in the wheelchair. It feels weird being pushed by Mom along the street—much weirder than in the hospital. I feel like a toddler in a stroller, as if I've grown down instead of up. We reach a street we need to cross, and the wheelchair jerks on the big curb, tipping me so I nearly fall out.

"Mom!" I yell.

"I'm so sorry—I'm not used to this," she says. "We should have practiced more outside. The sidewalk isn't flat and easy, like in the hospital."

I hate feeling so dependent and powerless. "I'm getting out," I tell her, standing up. "Just to cross the street."

It must look very odd to anyone passing, to see me stand up, walk quickly across the street, and then sit down in the wheelchair again.

At last we reach the theater, where I am welcomed like a celebrity. There's even a long red carpet, and everyone makes me feel very special.

"We have a ramp, so you'll be able to get on to the stage," a woman tells me.

"It's okay—I can walk, just not very far," I explain. Again, I know it will look weird to all these people here who've seen me in this wheelchair. They'll think I'm a fraud, but I don't really care.

I am invited to sit on a chair on the stage while an actor reads the opening of my story. Listening to it, I feel an urge to start writing again. The applause is thrilling, and, as I look out into the audience, I see that Dad is now sitting beside Mom and Miss Giles with the biggest grin on his face. I'm so happy he made it! When I'm given a glass trophy with my name engraved on it, I can even believe I'll be a real author one day.

The buzz of excitement has kept me going, but when it's

all over and Dad wheels me back to our car, I feel suddenly exhausted.

"Well done, Kasia!" says Miss Giles. "I hope you will be back at school soon."

"So do I," I tell her.

"I am so proud of you, *moje kochanie*!" Dad says. "We must go for a meal to celebrate. Maybe you will join us, Miss Giles?"

"That's kind of you to ask me, but I'll be off now," says Miss Giles. "I have lots of grading to do. And Kasia does look tired."

Mom shakes her head. "Takeout food at home," she suggests. "Look at her."

I agree—there's no way I could sit in a restaurant right now, and by the time we get home I am not up for takeout food, either. I just want to go to bed and am relieved to make it up the stairs. It was worth it, though—it has been one of the best days of my life.

"Should I do your curtains?" Mom offers, but I'm already halfway there.

"It's okay, Mom."

"This is a day I will never forget," she tells me, and I turn to meet her tired but smiling eyes. "Such an achievement!"

"It was good to get out of here—to do something so special, Mom. And I will get better. I know I will."

"You will," she tells me. "Sleep well, *mój aniele*."

I turn to pull the curtain closed as I listen to Mom's footsteps on the stairs. And I stop. She's there. The girl is there in the window. It's as if she's been waiting for me. She's staring straight at me—she's seen me, I'm sure. She looks solid—real—and she isn't vanishing. She looks so sad I feel a pang of guilt for having been out, having had such a good day. Then the curtains close across the street, and she disappears from view.

We are finally connected—the girl looking through her window and me through mine, even though we know nothing about each other. I lie in bed, sure now that she's no ghost. She's real. So what's going on? Why did the man and woman who live in the house say there is no girl there? And why does she never come out?

12

When I wake up the next morning, I feel a tingle of excitement that's not just left over from the awards. I'm still tired, but I am surprised and relieved that I don't feel too bad at all. In fact, I'm almost energetic! I feel determined to find out about the girl, and this time I'm not asking Mom—I'm going to go over to number 48 myself.

It's colder than the day before, and the chilly wind hits me as I come out of the front door, almost as if it's trying to warn me off. I pull my coat tight around me as I stand on the curb, checking for traffic before hurrying across. There's something reassuringly normal about walking out of the house and across the street, rather than being in a wheelchair like yesterday. I pause nervously in front of the door, but my legs are starting to ache, so I ring the bell. I hold my breath as I wait, listening. I hear the sound of a baby crying and it's coming nearer. I breathe out, trying to remember what I planned to say.

The woman opens the door and stands in the doorway with a chubby, wailing baby, about six months old, in her arms.

"Hi," I say awkwardly. "I live across the street."

"Oh, yes," she says. "Can I help you?" Her voice is not unfriendly, but there's something cagey about her expression. She shivers. "I don't want to stand here long—he's not too happy as you can see—and I don't want him catching cold." Her accent is strong, but her English is clear. She squeezes the baby and he wiggles and cries louder, like he's trying to escape.

"I...I just wondered..." I have to speak loudly to be heard over the baby's cries. "Is there a girl living here? Is she sick? I thought I saw her. I've been stuck at home—I'm not too well. I can't go to school, and I don't see many people. I just wondered if she'd maybe...like to meet up, maybe we could get to know each other? I've noticed she doesn't seem to go out. I wondered if she might be sick, like me, and it would be weird if the two of us are stuck inside being sick but living across from each other, if you know what I mean?"

I know I'm babbling, and my legs are now throbbing.

The woman's eyebrows have gone up. "Girl? Oh, you mean our niece? She's eighteen—not a girl like you. And she's not sick. She's staying with us and helping with the baby."

"But she doesn't go out?" I query.

The woman shrugs. "Not so often—she's a shy girl, prefers to stay at home. That is her choice. She's not in need of company. Is there anything else?"

"No. Sorry to bother you," I tell her. The front door quickly closes. I hurry back into the warmth of my own house and sit on the sofa. I don't even have the strength to take off my coat.

The girl exists. Finally, someone else has acknowledged her existence. Was she upstairs watching when I saw that young woman dragged into the car? I replay the scene in my mind, wondering what happened next, where they took her, where she is now—and whether she's okay. That girl is the only one who could verify what I saw. If only I could talk to her.

Two days later, I have to stay in bed again. The delayed reaction is so hard to understand, and it's like a kick in the teeth. It almost feels worse this time, because I used the wheelchair to help me on the day, but it hasn't stopped this from happening. It isn't fair.

I lie in bed thinking about the girl. When I stood there, at the door of number 48, I believed the woman was telling me the truth, but now I am starting to feel suspicious again. I feel like something's wrong in that house, though I can't really say why.

Why did the man tell Mom there was no girl? Was it because he thought of "girl" as "child" and this girl is eighteen, which might mean "woman" to him? She didn't look eighteen to me. And why didn't they mention her to the police?

If she isn't interested in making contact, if she's happy and busy, then why was she looking out of the window with such an unhappy expression? I can't help having the worst thoughts about why she's there. What if she's been kidnapped and is being held there against her will? What if she was abducted, like the woman I saw—and she's being held in that house and no one knows? No one, except me. The thought of it nags at me—it won't leave my head. I know it's unlikely—but what if it's true and I've known all this time but done nothing about it?

When I feel up to it, I browse online in short spurts. I find a website called Missing People with a section on missing kids. I scroll down through the photos—so many children it scares me. Some are probably teenagers who've run away. Some look really young, though. What has happened to them? They must be somewhere. I glance for a few seconds at each face, as if I'll be able to find out their secrets. I look at the boys as well as the girls. It feels wrong to miss anyone out—as if I'm saying that child is less important.

I find pictures of two Asian girls who *could* be the girl in the window. I try to think back to when I first saw her. Is it three months ago? One has only been missing for a month, so it can't be her. The other missing girl is named Farah Aziz. She is fifteen and has been missing for almost five months. She's from London, too. She looks a little angry in this picture, whereas the girl I see looks sadder, but the shape of her face, the dark hair—it really could be her. I search for her name and find a Facebook page dedicated to her, begging her to come home. There's a quote from her mother saying, "We can work it out."

My breath catches in my throat as I remember the reason I spotted the girl in the first place—the woman being dragged into the car. Maybe something like that happened to Farah?

She might have been there all these months, and I've been watching out of the window and she's been waiting—hoping I would rescue her and wondering why I keep looking out and looking out and yet doing nothing.

There is a number on the website. Do I dare I call it?

I decide I need to get a better look at her first—so I can be sure.

When the doorbell rings, she pushes me into the back room. She takes the baby, rocking him in her arms, and she shuts the door on me.

"Stay there," she barks.

The baby cries instantly. He cries for me, and I feel my heart wrench for him. I want his warmth, his comfort, as much as he wants mine.

I hear her voice as she opens the front door, sounding so different from the voice she uses for me, or even for him. She is polite and calm. I strain to hear what she's saying, what is being said to her, but I cannot grasp the words. The baby's noise is loud, and my English is not so good. I wish I dared open the door, just a crack, to hear better. But I dare not.

Then I hear the door shut and the baby's cries coming nearer, and I stand back before she comes into the room, her face blank and cold.

She hands the baby back to me, and his crying stops instantly.

Only I can settle him when he cries. Only I can tell his cries apart—the one for food and the one for hugs and the one for a clean diaper. She knows that. He is all that makes me human and not a ghost—the touch of his soft, soft skin, his small fingers tightly wrapped around mine, his eyes that follow me.

"We told you before—stay away from the windows," she tells me. "There are bad people out there. You want them to see you?"

Then she's gone.

13

I am still stuck upstairs and mainly in bed. I haven't even been well enough to sit by the window, so I have no idea if the girl has appeared again. I don't have the focus to study. I haven't even started the homework Ellie brought, I can't do the small amount of work that Judy left for me, and I can't even listen to audiobooks right now.

"I should have known those awards would be too much for you, *mój aniele*," Mom worries. She puts a mug of tea down on my bedside shelf and sighs.

"But it was amazing, Mom! I wanted to go, and I'm glad I went. I just wish I didn't feel so bad now."

"I know, you're right," Mom says, nodding. "Listen, I'm going to pop next door to check on Mrs. Gayatri. I won't be long. Will you be okay?"

"Of course, Mom," I say. "Tell her I'll visit myself as soon as I can."

"I'll tell her," Mom assures me.

Mom really isn't gone for long, and she comes straight upstairs to see me when she's back.

"How's Mrs. G.?" I ask her.

"Not too bad," Mom tells me. "Her daughter's there—seems very nice. They were chatting away as if they'd never been apart. I've never seen Mrs. G. so animated. I met the grandson, too. Navin—Nav, he likes to be called. He must be about your age."

"What's he like?" I ask.

"I don't know. He didn't say much—sat playing on his phone, with earphones in. Mrs. Gayatri says he's offered to work on her yard this week, since he's on a break from school, so that's good. She hasn't been able to really look after it for years. I did suggest to your dad once that he might mow it for her and he said he would when he had a chance, but of course he's never gotten around to it, and he's so busy at work."

Later I come out of the bathroom and hear the sound of the lawn mower out back. I am curious and make my way to my parents' bedroom, clutching the walls as I go, so I can look out the window. I sit on the dressing-table stool and peer down into Mrs. G.'s yard.

I can see a boy with pale brown skin and dark brown hair sticking out from under a red hat. He is mowing the overgrown lawn with Mrs. Gayatri's mower, but is doing it in the most bizarre way I have ever seen. He's walking in zigzags, criss-crossing, sometimes going around in small circles. It's almost like a lawn mower waltz or something! I find myself laughing out loud, I can't help it. He's thorough, though, and it does look much neater when he's finished.

Next day I'm happy to see he's there again. This time he's on a stepladder, trying to cut some dead wood out of an evergreen hedge with shears. The hedge is taking on a very weird shape, and I start to wonder if he's actually doing topiary. I'm glad I can remember the word for it—I remember Dad once describing hedges shaped like amazing birds in the garden of a big mansion he was remodeling. He showed me pictures online. Nav's hedge is starting to look like some kind of dinosaur, with a long, curved back and spindly tail. Just as I think he's about to start work on the head, he chops it off, so maybe it wasn't meant to be a dinosaur after all.

"Nav seems like a nice boy," says Mom, coming in with a pile of washing. "He's working so hard out there. Maybe I'll suggest he comes over for a slice of cake and a drink. Wouldn't you like to meet him, Kasia?"

I wasn't expecting this. "Mom! There's no way I can make it downstairs. Are you suggesting some strange boy comes up to my bedroom—with me in my pajamas? I don't think so."

Mom laughs at my expression. "Kasia, don't be silly! You're bored and stuck indoors, and I'm sure he could do with a break. You're curious about him, I can see, or you wouldn't have made the effort to walk all the way in here to look out the back window. I will help you get dressed."

"In sweatpants and a hoodie?"

"Well, you're not going on a date, are you? That'll be fine for a chat and a snack."

"You can suggest it to Mrs. Gayatri if you want," I say, sighing. "He'll probably say no anyway."

But he doesn't. Mom goes next door later that afternoon and comes back saying Nav will pop in tomorrow.

Now I'm feeling so nervous. Why did I agree? What are we going to talk about? I don't even know what time he's coming.

The next morning I get dressed slowly, the first time in a long time, and then lie down for an hour. When I get up, I look at myself in the mirror and try to cover up the spots that have flared up on my face. I brush my hair. It's so dry. It needs conditioner, but I don't have the energy to wash it very often, and Mom has to help me.

He doesn't come. I wonder if he's changed his mind. I imagine him sitting with his earphones in, listening to music, playing some game on his phone. I'm sure he'd rather be doing that than coming over here to visit me. He must have just said yes to be polite.

Then the doorbell rings. I hear Mom greeting Nav cheerfully, but I don't hear his reply. I think about sitting in the chair, but decide to leave it for Nav. As I hear the footsteps on the stairs, I prop myself up with pillows.

"Come and meet Kasia," Mom says brightly, opening the bedroom door. She stands holding it open and Nav comes in.

He's shorter than I thought—shorter than me—and he looks so nervous, as if I'm lying here dying or something. I'm only sick—I shouldn't be that terrifying.

"Can I get you a drink?" Mom asks him. "A piece of apple cake?"

"I..."

"I'll bring you some," Mom doesn't let him finish. "Do you want anything, Kasia?"

"No thanks, Mom."

"Sit down, then, and I'll leave you to get to know each other."

Mom's gone. Nav sits awkwardly on the edge of the chair and I look at him. My room suddenly feels even smaller with this strange boy sitting here so close to me.

"Thanks for coming," I say, though I'm not sure if I mean it yet.

"S'all right, not much else to do." He shrugs but doesn't look up.

I wait for him to speak, but he clearly doesn't have a clue what to say.

"I saw you mowing the lawn," I comment.

He looks startled. "I thought you were stuck in here?"

"It varies from day to day," I tell him. "Some days I can get downstairs and others I am stuck in bed. I can get to the bathroom next door, and sometimes I make it to my parents' bedroom."

"So you were spying on me?"

I'm not sure if he's teasing or if he's really embarrassed.

I nod and smile. "Interesting way to mow a lawn! You never done one before?"

"No. We don't have a yard. I was just having a little bit of fun. Looks all right, though, doesn't it?"

"Yeah, it looks fine. You did a good job."

He meets my eyes for the first time.

"I'd love to have a yard," he says. "I got a Saturday job at the garden center near where we live—just watering the plants and that—I thought it would be boring, but I really like it. I'm getting to know all the names and what soil different plants like. I want to study it—plants, garden design, and all that."

I have no interest in plants whatsoever, so I have never thought that someone might want to study them. I don't know anyone else my age that's interested in gardening.

"So maybe you take after your grandmother," I say. "She loves her garden."

"I know. Hey, listen... I wanted to thank you—for finding Nani, you know? Saving her life. If it wasn't for you, I'd never have gotten to meet her."

Mom's head appears around the door. "Here. Enjoy, Navin!" She hands over a plate with a large piece of apple cake and a fork.

"Thanks—that looks great," he tells her.

"You taste—tell me what you think," says Mom, and she's gone.

There's an awkward silence. Nav takes a bite of cake and brushes the crumbs from his mouth. I can see from his eyes he is more impressed than he expected to be with Mom's cake.

"So, you didn't even know your grandmother existed?" I blurt out.

Nav shrugs again and stares down at his plate. "I knew she existed, and I knew Mom never wanted to talk about her, that's all."

"Sorry, I shouldn't have asked," I say—though I'm hoping he will go on.

He doesn't.

"What's actually wrong with you then?" he suddenly asks. "You don't look sick."

I'm a little stunned by the question. I thought I was being too personal, but now he is. Maybe he's deliberately getting his own back.

"I mean," he goes on, "Nani told me it was ME, but I don't really know what that is."

"It stands for myalgic encephalomyelitis, and it started with a bad case of tonsillitis," I explain. "I never fully recovered. As soon as I do anything that requires any effort, I go backward again. The pain in my legs, the pain I feel after walking, the dizziness, the swollen glands in my neck, the tiredness after doing the smallest thing—none of that shows. It's invisible. And I've been like this for eight months."

"That's a long time," he says.

I nod. "I hate that I'm missing so much school, and that my friends are busy going on with their lives and I'm not—it's like someone's pressed the pause button."

"So, what do you do all day?" he asks.

"Listen to the podcasts, audiobooks, look out of the window, try to study a little when I can, think of ideas for stories I want to write."

"You write stories?"

"Yes—I won a competition. That's the trophy." I point at it on my desk, a little worried that I sound like I'm bragging.

Nav strokes the trophy and looks genuinely impressed. "Nice," he says. "I'm not really a book person, me. I prefer movies, you know? But you need to get out of here, girl. It can't be right being stuck indoors. Maybe you could sit outside and watch me gardening?"

I try not to laugh. I can't say that watching him weeding Mrs. G.'s garden is much of an incentive, though I think he meant it nicely.

"I need time to recover from that award ceremony last week for the writing competition," I tell him. "What do you do when you're not gardening?"

"There's this game I play online—I play people all over the world."

He starts to describe the game and I feel myself drifting off.

Nav suddenly stops. "Hey—you look like you need a rest! Sorry, I was going on and on. I hope I haven't made you feel worse?"

"No. It was nice of you to come," I tell him. "I hope you'll come again."

14

Ellie comes over on her own the next day, and I'm glad to have my best friend to myself again.

"What's new?" she asks.

"Not much," I shrug. "Mrs. G. next door—her daughter and grandson have come to stay. He's our age—he came over here yesterday."

"What's he like?" Ellie asks eagerly.

"He's into gardening!" I tell her.

"Oh!" She makes a face. "But he's tall and handsome?"

"Not tall—shorter than me. He was friendly enough though," I add.

"Too bad," says Ellie. "Bet you'd rather have Josh staying next door!"

I laugh.

"So the award ceremony knocked you out?" she says. "It's such a shame. That trophy is so beautiful!"

"It was an amazing day," I say, nodding, "but I wish I didn't have to suffer for it afterward."

"You were doing so well. I thought you'd be back at school soon," Ellie comments. "I wish they'd just find a pill you could take and that would be it—you'd be cured."

"I wish that, too," I say with a sigh.

"Isn't there anything they can do?"

"Not much. I have to wait and see what the consultant says when I eventually see him."

"Maybe you need a vacation—somewhere in the sun?" Ellie suggests. "We're going to Spain in the summer, the same villa we went to last year. It's amazing, the pool is fab. Swimming might do you good, too. Hey! Maybe you could come with us?"

"I'd love to, Ell—I'd love to so much—but I could never manage it. Think about how I've been since that short trip to the award ceremony. I could never cope with a trip to Spain—the airport, the plane, the journey at the other end, or the heat. I'd be laid up in bed feeling terrible and I'd have to shut all the blinds—the light would be so bright, and I wouldn't feel well enough to even sit up." Tears well up, and I can't stop them sliding down my cheeks.

"Oh, Kasia. I'm so sorry! I didn't mean to make you cry!"

"I can't believe I'll ever get better. Maybe I'll never be able to go on a plane again. Maybe I'll never graduate from college. Maybe I'll never be able to work or marry Josh or have kids or anything."

"Stop, stop!" Ellie holds out her arms to hug me. I let her, even though the hug hurts my muscles. "You're *going* to get better, okay? Most people do, don't they?"

"Sorry, Ellie—just now and then it all builds up and I feel so frightened."

"You'll be okay," she tells me again. "You've got me as a friend—your BFF, don't forget that! And I'm sure you'll get married one day, if that's what you really want, but it might not be to Josh. Do you know anyone who married someone they went to school with? I don't! Not many people do, I bet. Look, why don't we watch a movie together—a funny one to cheer you up?"

"Thanks, Ellie. But I can't watch a screen for more than five minutes without getting a headache."

I see Ellie's face drop, and I force a smile. "Anyway—enough!" I say. "Let's talk about something else before I drown in self-pity! There's something I've been meaning to tell you."

"Go on," she says.

At last I tell her about the abduction, about the girl in the window, how the man and woman living there seem to be lying—even my mad ghost theory! Finally, I show her the picture of Farah on the missing persons website.

Ellie's eyes are wide with astonishment as she peers at my tablet. "So you really think this could be her—and that she's being kept across the street against her will?"

I nod. "I think it's possible."

"Are you going to call the police—or this missing persons hotline?" she asks.

"I don't feel sure enough," I tell Ellie. "The police didn't believe me about the abduction. I don't want to make a fool of myself."

Ellie walks over to the window. "She isn't there now," she says.

"I haven't seen her since I went across the street and asked," I admit. "Maybe they're not letting her near the window. Or maybe she is eighteen and busy with the baby, like the woman said."

"Next time you should take a picture with your phone," says Ellie. "Then you can zoom in and take a closer look. And maybe there's another way to communicate with her. Could you put a note through the door?"

I shake my head. "If the man or woman found it, they'd never give it to her—and they would know I didn't believe them," I say. "But the photo's a good idea. I'll try that."

"What else, what else...?" Ellie says thoughtfully. "How about Morse code? You could use the flashlight on your phone."

"I don't know Morse code," I say doubtfully. "And she might not, either."

"You can look it up online. It's worth a try."

"I guess." I nod again. "Thanks, Ellie—I'm glad I told you."

After Ellie leaves, I look up Morse code and write out the signals for "Do you need help?" I sit and watch at the window for as long as I can, but there's no sign of the girl.

15

The next day, Nav comes over with a book. It's called *Recovering from Chronic Fatigue.* I thank him and put it on my desk. Mom got a few books out of the library when I was diagnosed, but they weren't much help. This one looks better, but it's a heavy book, and I know it will give me pains in my arms if I hold it for too long. Whoever wrote or published it didn't think about that! It's nice of him, though.

"My mom spotted it in that used bookshop on Main Street," he tells me. "And I've been reading it myself. Just call me Dr. Navin—here to get you well!"

I laugh a little, but I'm also surprised. He's been reading it—to help me. That's thoughtful and kind.

"I won't need to read it then," I joke. "It's too heavy anyway."

"No, it's really easy to read," he tells me.

"I mean the weight of it, not the content!"

He laughs. "Rest it on your pillow!"

"So, what's the advice, doc?"

"It's all about routine," Nav says. "You do the same things every day—only half of what you're able to do, what you can do without feeling worse. Then you very, very gradually increase that over time. It's all about recharging your batteries. Like your illness has made them flat, and they need to be charged. Light activity will begin to recharge them."

"Sounds like the pacing I already do," I say.

"But it's not regular, is it? I think you do much more some days and then you're laid up afterward. Isn't that right?"

"Yes. When there are things I really want to do—you know, like the writing award ceremony. I know I'll suffer afterward, but it's worth it."

"I think you should try the suggestions in this book—along with my help, of course. If you do it gradually, it should stop you from having so many setbacks. And I prescribe that spending time outside in the fine weather, watching me gardening next door, will be the best treatment ever!"

"It's not exactly fine, the weather," I say, looking out at the cloudy sky.

"But it will get better!" he assures me. "It's pretty warm today—no chill in the air. Come on."

"What, *now*?"

"No time like the present, as my mother always says when she wants me to clean my room!"

"I am feeling a little bit better today. I was thinking about going downstairs. But..."

"No buts. You have a hoodie or something?"

I'm wearing sweatpants and a T-shirt. "I thought you said it was warm."

"Warm if you dress right. Come on. Take my arm if you want."

"No, it's okay. I can manage."

I find myself on my feet, grabbing my jacket from the closet and pulling it on. I follow Nav down the stairs and for once manage to not pause for breath halfway. I worry instantly—is that a good thing or have I overdone it already?

Nav opens the front door.

"I need to tell Mom I'm going out," I protest.

"It's done—she knows," he says, and before I can object to the fact that they've been conspiring together, I am outside.

I follow Nav around to the garden gate next door and into the backyard. There's still a chill wind, but I like the feel of the sun on my back when it peeks out from behind the clouds. As I stand on the patio, my legs begin to ache and I look around anxiously for a bench or a small wall to perch on. There's nothing.

"Nav—I don't think... I need to sit down. I'd better go back."

"No need—I'll have a chair out of the shed in two secs. Should have done that first!" He jogs across the grass and returns with a lawn chair, which he quickly unfolds for me.

Now that I'm sitting and not panicking, I can really look at the yard. The lawn is fine now, but although Nav's done some pruning, there are still lots of overgrown and unwieldy shrubs. Long, wispy branches swing wildly in the gentle breeze as if they are looking for something to hold on to. A few daffodils have opened and some flowering bushes are stretching up to find light, like children trying to see over a wall.

"It looks like it needs a lot of work," I say.

"You're right," Nav agrees, but he says it cheerfully and not downheartedly, like I might do if confronted by a challenge like this.

"I wish I was here for longer so I could really get into it," he says. "Nani's shown me photos from years ago, when my grandfather was still alive. They both loved this garden, and it was beautiful. Would you like to see?"

"Sure," I nod.

Nav is quiet for a moment.

"You look sad," I tell him.

"Just thinking about how weird, but great it is getting to know my grandmother, and wishing I could have met my grandfather. Do you have grandparents?"

I shake my head. "I did—in Poland. *Babcia*, my gran, was the only one I met, and she died last year. I was sad, but I didn't know her well—visiting once or twice a year wasn't enough to get very close. Mom was really upset, though."

I pause, then blurt out a question that I'm sure Mom

would say was too personal. "If you don't mind me asking, what about your dad?"

Nav shrugs. "Never knew him—my grandparents didn't approve since he wasn't a Hindu, so Mom took off with him and cut contact with them. She was sort of a rebel, my mom. Then, when she found out she was pregnant, my dad went off and left her. I've never felt like I needed to try to find him 'cause he clearly had no interest in me. Mom didn't feel like crawling back to her parents, so she stayed away. Now that she's back with Nani, she regrets their falling-out and all the time they lost, especially since they're getting along so well!"

"Something good came out of your gran's stroke then?"

"Yes—and that's thanks to you, isn't it?" He smiles. He looks down toward the back of the yard.

"Now, can I take you on a tour?" he asks me.

"Tour?" I look down the yard which stretches to at least thirty yards. "I'm not...I can't..."

"Negativity!" he interrupts. "The enemy of progress and recovery."

"It's not negativity, it's realism," I argue. "If I overdo it, I relapse. That's a fact that I've learnt from experience."

"Who's talking about overdoing it?"

"A tour—that's what you said."

"A tour of the patio!" He grins.

"Oh. You should have said."

"You must worry less, Kasia. Anxiety is also your enemy.

Can I get you a drink? Are you warm enough? I can fetch one of Nani's blankets for your knees?"

He's seen me shudder slightly at the breeze.

"Please stop fussing, Nav. I'm okay." I can't stand the thought of sitting with a blanket over my knees like an old lady. I'm beginning to wish I'd stayed at home, but once Nav starts some frenetic pruning, I can't help laughing and he clearly enjoys having an audience.

When he's finished, we walk around the patio. I have to sit down again after a couple of minutes, but he continues talking, telling me his plans for the garden. I have no idea what plants he's talking about, but I love his enthusiasm for it all.

Mrs. G. comes out later, bringing her photos to show me. Nav fetches another chair for her.

"My garden is helping to tear my grandson away from his video games," she says with a smile.

"Nah, I can do both," Nav teases her. "Garden all day, game all night."

I look at the photos and am amazed to see an exotic-looking, flower-filled garden. "It's incredible! It doesn't look like the same garden!"

"We tried to re-create the gardens of our childhoods in India," she tells me. "Of course, many of the plants there won't grow here, but we went for the bright colors we loved."

"I'd love to restore it," says Nav. "School vacations don't

give you enough time to do a perfect job, but least I can make a start."

"Where's your daughter?" I ask Mrs. G. "Doesn't she want to sit outside, too?"

"Devi's next door," she tells me, "chatting with your mother."

When I come home, I find them sitting in our kitchen eating cake. I immediately like the look of Devi, and I can see she has the same smile as Mrs. G.

"Hi, you must be Kasia," Devi says cheerfully. "My mom told me about your mother's cakes, and she's right. Your mom's a talented baker. She should be entering the *Bake-Off* on TV!"

"Sit with us, Kasia—try some," says Mom, smiling. I really want to go and lie down, but I decide to stay for a minute.

"Just a small piece, Mom," I say. "Is it one of Gran's mystery recipes?"

"Yes—it's poppy seed cake. It's not as good as Gran's, though."

I sit and she places a small piece on a plate in front of me. I take a bite.

"It's delicious, Mom."

I look from Mom to Devi. Mom is looking happier and

more animated than I've seen her for a long time. It occurs to me how isolated she must have been feeling, cut off from her friends at work and stuck at home, caring for me. I like Devi, and Mom clearly does, too. Devi has a vibrancy, an energy about her, even though she's sitting still. She's wearing a top covered in colorful flowers—red, purple, and orange, like the photo of Mrs. G.'s garden. I think she will be a good friend for Mom.

That evening, as I'm closing the curtains, I look out—and I see her. The girl. The room behind her is dark, but she's there and she doesn't vanish.

I grab my phone and unfold the paper on the windowsill where I've written the Morse code. Using the flashlight, I flash the signal for *Do you need help?*, and I have to concentrate hard to make sure I do it right.

By the time I've finished, she's gone. I wonder if she understood any of it. Maybe she's gone to get a flashlight—or her phone or iPad to look up what it means. She'll have to come back.

I wait and wait but she doesn't come. Maybe flickering lights give her a headache, like they do with some people with ME. Or maybe she can't cope with the light at all. A vampire? I can't help laughing at myself for having this thought. I just wish I knew what was going on.

She shone a light. What was she was doing? Flashing and flashing. She must not do this. She mustn't. Was she trying to say something?

Later I think maybe it is a code. A code with lights—I think I have heard of such a thing. But I have no flashlight to reply, no way to look up any code. Maybe it isn't a code.

Yet I am happy that she knows I am here. She cares. Maybe she only wants to tell me that there is light—that this darkness will one day end. I hope she is right.

16

I am out in Mrs. G.'s garden with Nav. It's a Saturday in March, and the garden is scattered with daffodils. Nav is planting bulbs that he says will come up in the summer. He seems to have stacks of them. I look at the labels and pictures.

"Will they really look like this?" I ask. "It'll be amazing."

"I hope so!" says Nav, grinning. "Come and see the magnolia. It's half-hidden but the flowers are beautiful already."

He has pruned back some of the bushes a little, but enough so that when I stop and look through the gap, I can see a tree in a clearing, clustered with pink flowers.

I reach for a low-hanging blossom and breathe in. "It's like perfume," I tell him. Then the scent catches my throat and I have to step away. I can't even tolerate nice smells these days.

"I want to grow lots of herbs and vegetables, too," Nav tells me. "And I'll plant more stuff at the end of May—when there's no risk of frost. Nani's been sharing her knowledge—and a couple of good gardening books, too! I've got a lot to learn, though."

"You'll be back in May then?" I ask.

"Yes, and most weekends, too, maybe more. My mom's getting all emotional about Nani, saying we should come and look after her," Nav tells me. "They are getting along so well I don't think they want to be apart. They want to make up for lost time."

"What—move in?" He nods.

"Do you want to?" I ask.

He shrugs. "I've got friends where we're living, but it's a small apartment. Nani's garden—that makes it tempting... Oh and having you next door, of course!"

I make a face.

"What? You don't want your 'doctor' living next door?" he teases.

I try to imagine what it would be like having Nav living next door. I've never had a neighbor my age.

"Oh—I'd probably have to go to your school, too," he says. "What's it like?"

"Can hardly remember—haven't been there for a long time!" I comment. "But if you do end up there, I can tell you who to avoid and that kind of stuff."

He smiles. "Thanks."

"If you stay, which bedroom will be yours—is it at the front, like mine?"

"Yes—that's where I'm sleeping now," he tells me.

"Have you ever seen anyone across the street, looking out the window?" I ask.

He shakes his head. "I don't look out much," he says. "Why?"

"Can I tell you something," I ask, "something a little weird?"

"Go on," he says, looking intrigued.

I tell him about the girl and why I'm worried about her. I tell him how the couple denied she existed and then said she was their eighteen-year-old niece. I tell him about the abduction I saw and how I think the girl saw, too. I don't tell him I thought she was a ghost.

"It does sound odd," he says. "I haven't seen her, but I'll have to keep a look out."

"I keep worrying about her," I explain, "and then telling myself she must be okay because all the things I'm imagining—that she's been kidnapped or something like that—seem too far-fetched. But I really want to know the truth."

"Maybe you could wait until the couple go out and then try again," Nav suggests. "You could go and knock, see if she'll come to the door and speak to you. Then you'll get a good look at her and find out if she's okay. And you can ask her about that woman and the car—whether she saw anything."

"I could," I say. "It can't do any harm to try."

"I'll come with you, if you want?" says Nav.

"Really? Thanks."

"I'll give you my number, and you can text me when you know the people are out. If I'm free, I'll come."

For the rest of the day and on Sunday I keep an even closer watch on the house, until I finally see the couple come out, get into the white car, and drive off.

I text Nav.

"Meet out in front in five," he texts back.

It takes me more than five minutes, but Nav is waiting for me when I finally get there. We cross the street, and I ring the bell on the shabby red front door. "Keep an eye out," I tell him. "Just in case they come back."

There's no answer. I ring again. Then I look through the mailbox slot. Unlike Mrs. G.'s, there is no letter guard, just a hole. It is easier to see in, but there's nothing to see except two closed doors and the staircase.

"Is anyone there?" I call. "It's Kasia from across the street. I just want to know if you're okay."

We wait. "If she's there, I don't think she's coming," says Nav.

Then I hear a baby's cry. Nav's eyes shift to the right. He heard it, too.

"They didn't take the baby!" I explain. "I saw them go—and I didn't think about it. They left the baby here. So the girl must be in there. They can't have left the baby alone, can they?"

"Call again," says Nav. I do.

Still there is no answer apart from the distant baby cries.

"We'll have to leave it," Nav says, shaking his head. "Sometimes people just don't like answering the door."

I don't want to—but I know he's right, and my legs feel like they're going to give, anyway.

"We'll try again another time," Nav says.

She rang the bell. I did not know who it was. The door is locked—"to keep me safe." Bad people might come. Then I heard her voice. I heard her say, "It is Kasia—from across the street." So now I know her name, a pretty name, Kasia. She is my friend—my only friend, come to call for me.

How good it would be to open the door, to invite her in, to make tea and have cake and sit and chat with her, show her the baby, and she'd coo at him and squeeze his chubby legs.

She had someone with her. I heard her talking to someone. Trust no one. That's what they tell me. It was a male voice. Who was he? Maybe he is the bad person they spoke of. Maybe he's come to take me to another place—a far worse place than this.

It does not matter, because the door is locked. I have no key. Does she not realize—the girl, Kasia—that I have no key?

17

I don't want it to go to Nav's head, but I think the advice from the book he gave me is making a difference. I am able to come downstairs every day and even to do some of the work Judy has given me.

Nav has gone back home, but we text each other every day. I miss him being next door and am glad when he says he'll be back on Friday for the weekend.

He texts me as soon as he arrives, and I'm happy to be back out in the garden with him.

"Guess what? You are going to be seeing a lot more of me! We are moving here to live with Nani."

"Wow! That's great. Mrs. G. must be so happy!"

"And I hope you are, too!" he teases. "Mom was worried about me changing schools midway through the semester, but your school has assured her it will all be fine."

"So you'll be in my grade?"

“Yes. I’ll start after Easter. It would be better, of course, if you were there to show me around.”

“I wish I could.”

We’re both quiet for a moment. I won’t be able to show him around at school, but I think I’m going to like having him next door.

“You can tell me things I need to know, and I’ll tell you what’s going on,” he says. “And you will be back there soon. That is Dr. Nav’s ambition!”

“Mine too!” I tell him.

“For now, though, I need your help with this garden.”

I look at him doubtfully. “Wait here.”

He hurries to the house and comes back with what looks like a magazine.

“Plant catalog,” he says, handing it to me. “I want to plant new flowering shrubs and rescue as many as I can from what’s here. I’ve already planted bulbs, and I plan to sow seeds on a big scale so there will be an amazing display of flowers for the summer. Gran says I can get a mini-greenhouse—a plastic one—so I can grow some seeds there now and transplant the seedlings in May. I will get some plant plugs, too—small plants, ready to go right in the ground.”

“What do you want me to do?” I ask. I flip through, and beautiful flowers leap from the pages. I have no idea what most of them are.

“You can help me choose. Anything colorful or

exotic-looking. You know the kind of thing Nani likes. While I edge the border, you take this pen and circle anything you like."

I feel a wonderful sense of calm as I browse through the catalog, glancing up frequently to watch Nav chopping the border with an edging tool. He does not seem to like straight lines and is curving it in a very attractive way. A robin is sitting on the fence watching, too, and a few other birds are twittering cheerfully by the bird feeder. It really is starting to feel like spring now, and I feel a renewed optimism.

"I need a drink," he tells me. He goes in and brings out two glasses of juice, then sits down beside me.

"Seen anything you like?" he asks.

"I like these rudbeckias—and the dahlias," I tell him.

"Good choices—I love them, too." He grins. "I want to get a bench, too, with an awning over it, so Nani can relax where there is warm sun, but also a little shade. I'm watching on auction sites, and Mom has said she'll pay if I can find one that's not too expensive."

"I like the way you've done the edge of the border—all curvy," I comment. "It looks much nicer than when it was just straight."

"I saw it in this garden book. It shows you how to add mirrors to make it look even bigger. That's something I'm thinking about."

"I can't wait to see it in the summer," I say.

"I can picture it so clearly in my mind," Nav replies. "I hope I can make it happen."

"I'm sure you can," I say.

I last for a whole two hours in the garden, before I have to go home and lie down for a while. I even do some studying in the evening. I'm so happy Nav is moving in next door, but a little bit of me is worried that they may have given him my place at school because they think I won't be coming back. Inside, I hope that's just me thinking the worst again.

On Monday, Ellie and Lia come by on their way back from rehearsals, full of the show—which is just before the Easter break, less than two weeks away—and how brilliant it is going to be.

"You will come, won't you?" Ellie demands. "You're so much better now."

I discuss it with Mom and Dad. They agree in the end that I can go to the show but come right home afterward. Dad will drive me and I'm to call him to pick me up the moment it ends.

I mention to Nav that I'm going and to my surprise he asks if he can come, too. I'm not sure how I feel about that—I'm happy for him to come, but I know that one of the reasons I want to go is to see Josh. I hope that won't be too obvious.

On the day, I make an effort with jeans and a nice top I

haven't worn for nearly a year. I manage to wash my hair and Mom blow-dries it for me.

"There, you look almost human!" she teases.

I look in the mirror and am happy with what I see. Even my skin is looking healthier.

Dad and Nav both compliment me on how I look. Dad drives me and Nav to school and is full of reminders about calling when it finishes so he can pick me up. We pass the staircase where I panicked last time I was here, all those months ago, and I glance up at it. I'm sure I could manage those stairs now, but I'm still glad the show is on the ground floor.

I sit with Nav in the second row. Some people give me strange looks—maybe they're surprised to see me, or they wonder who this boy is that I'm with. Bethany and Amy from my grade come up smiling, saying it's nice to see me. I'm surprised, because they've never been that friendly.

Then they sit two rows behind, and I can hear them whispering loudly about me. "Thought she was sick? She looks fine." I don't turn to look, but I know that's Amy's voice. "How come she's well enough for a show and not well enough for school?"

"Too right!" That's Bethany. "Anyway, my dad says there's no such things as ME. It's all in your head."

Nav gives me a look. He's heard them, too, and looks as if he's going to say something back.

I shake my head. "They're not my friends," I tell him. "Just ignore them."

"I hope they're not all like that here," says Nav.

Before I can reply, Miss Giles comes over, saying she's pleased to see me not needing a wheelchair and hopes I'll be back at school soon. She talks enthusiastically about the award again, and I start to feel better.

Then Erin and Tilly, who I thought *were* my friends, but who I haven't seen for months, shuffle over to say hi.

"Good to see you!" Erin tells me. "I'm sorry I haven't been in touch. I'm pretty useless around sick people."

I'm not sure what to say to this, so instead I introduce them to Nav and they start talking to him. The seats are hard, and, although it's embarrassing, I'm glad Mom made me bring a cushion. I wouldn't have lasted three minutes otherwise.

A few more people come over to say hi and tell me how well I'm looking.

"Seem like a friendly bunch," Nav says, "apart from those two losers behind us."

I nod. I almost feel like a fraud, I feel so normal. Maybe I will be back at school sooner than I thought. The lights go down and the concert begins. To my delight, I am close to where Josh is sitting in the orchestra and I have a perfect view of him. I keep hoping he'll glance up and see me. If he'd only look at me—meet my eyes, give me a friendly wink or nod or smile—it would completely make my day. But he doesn't. He's really focused on the music and concentrating with every breath.

Ellie and Lia have small roles in the show, but perform them impressively and are clearly enjoying themselves.

"Wow! That was so good!" I tell Ellie, when she comes out. I introduce Nav, and she says hi.

She looks at her watch. "It isn't even late, there's a party now—the after-show party. Will you come—just for a little while? Nav, you'll stay, too, won't you?"

Nav hesitates. "It's up to you, Kasia. I'll stay if you want to."

I glance around to see Josh putting his violin in its case. I don't have the energy or nerve to go over now, though I'd love to tell him how good the show was, how good *he* was. I imagine him smiling, his whole face lighting up as I speak.

Feeling a little guilty, I turn back to Nav. "Just for a few minutes," I agree. "I don't want to overdo it."

"Great, come on then," says Nav. "You can introduce me to some more people."

Nav and I follow Ellie, leaving Josh still packing up his violin and talking to some classmates.

We reach the cafeteria, where the party is being held. The room's been cleared and there aren't many chairs. My worst fear is that there will be nowhere to sit down. I am still clutching my cushion and get a few odd glances. I want to put the cushion on a chair and sit on it as quickly as possible.

"Nav..." I begin, but I don't even need to finish, since he's there with a chair he's grabbed from somewhere. I just hope he didn't tip anyone off it in his haste.

"Thanks," I say.

He grins. "I'll get us some drinks." He turns to Ellie. "What would you like?"

He goes off to get Ellie a soda and me some water, and Ellie watches him, chuckling.

"What?" I demand.

"It's like he thinks he's your nurse or something—fussing over you like that. Don't you find him annoying?"

I feel instantly irritated with Ellie. "No, I don't," I say firmly.

More people are coming in, and the room is getting crowded. I'm starting to feel hot and a little dizzy. I'm relieved when Nav comes back with the drinks.

We chat with Ellie, Tia, and Erin, and I introduce Nav to a few boys from our class. Then the others go off to mingle, and I'm left with Nav.

"I hope I can get back to playing the cello," I tell him. "I should have been in this show. I loved being in the orchestra."

"I'd really like to hear you play," says Nav.

"I want to get back to playing, but I can't even lift it now," I say.

"One day you will," he assures me. "Maybe you'll even play in next year's concert."

"I'm getting stronger all the time," I say, nodding.

He gives me a sweet smile, and I smile back.

Then I see Josh has come in. There is a kind of aura

around him, an energy that's almost like a beam of light. For a moment he's on his own, looking around. I wonder if he'll see me. I want to get up and go over to him, but I don't dare—what if he doesn't remember me at all?

Then a girl goes up to him. They're talking. I don't know her name, but she's in the same grade as Josh. He's smiling and nodding. Is he with her? Are they together?

"So?"

Nav has asked me something, and I've missed it completely.

"What? Sorry?"

"I think maybe we should go now? Are you going to text your dad?"

I look at my watch and notice with horror that it's after eleven. How did that happen? I pull out my phone and see three unread messages and three missed calls from my dad. He's not going to be happy. And I am right. He is furious when he arrives—with Nav as well as me.

"I'm so sorry," Nav tells him as we get in the car. "But I think Kasia's fine. I've been looking after her. She's been sitting down the whole time."

"I think I'm okay, Dad," I tell him. "I had fun—I almost felt normal for the first time in months. Please don't be angry."

"We said clearly that you could go, but to text me right after," Dad reminds me. "There was no mention of a party! We would never have agreed to that. Why do you ignore us? We say it for good reason—for your health!"

Dad sounds so disappointed, I feel horrible. I hate letting him down.

"I didn't mean to ignore your messages. I just... I mean, I lost track of time. I'm sure I'll be okay, though—I feel fine."

"We'll see," says Dad. "I hope you're right."

Nav gives me a big smile and squeezes my hand before he goes. "I'll see you tomorrow."

I walk quickly upstairs to bed, eager to show Dad that I am fine. My legs are actually not too bad, and I am buzzing with excitement. Normal life, school, friends—everything that's felt so far away suddenly feels much closer.

18

The next day, when I wake up, I check my body for pain. Legs—some pain, but not too bad, arms—the same. Head pretty clear. I sit up gingerly and then stand. I am okay. Not perfect, but no major relapse. I am delighted.

Nav texts to check I'm okay and I'm relieved to tell him I feel fine.

"See—your dad was wrong! Going to the show was good for you," he tells me. "As well as giving me the chance to meet lots of people before I start at your school."

"I wish I was ready to start back, too," I reply. "But at least it feels like it will be possible one day."

The following day I wake up and find I can't move at all. I am too weak to sit up, and my legs are throbbing. I feel completely wiped out. It's a delayed reaction, and I should have known it would happen. Why do I never learn? And I hate that Dad was right.

I can't walk. I can't get out of bed. And it's not just for one day. I'm worse than I was when I was bedbound before and I feel so depressed. It isn't fair. It just isn't fair.

I feel so bad I start to blame Nav for encouraging me. Even the fact that I saw Josh doesn't cheer me up anymore. Seeing him with that girl didn't help since they're probably going out together now. I feel helpless and so, so alone.

One night, Mom comes to check on me on her way to bed and I pretend to be asleep since I don't have the energy to speak or even open my eyes.

"Yes, she's asleep," she tells Dad. I hear their bedroom door close, but within minutes I can hear them arguing—and it's about me.

"We should never have let her go," says Dad. "Look what she's done to herself—and after all that progress!"

"It's understandable that she wants to do these things—to be with her friends," says Mom.

"But she knows full well what happens when she does too much. She has to take responsibility. And so do you. Why aren't you phoning the doctors, the hospital, to insist on some real treatment? You accept what the doctors tell you—you let her lie forgotten on a waiting list!"

"That's not fair," Mom protests. "I'm the one caring for her all day, every day. I gave up my job to do that. I want her healthy and back at school just as much as you do."

"Why is this happening to us?" Dad groans. "What have we done to deserve it? We move to this country, we both work hard to make a good life for our children. And all we have is one dropout, good-for-nothing son and a daughter who can't get out of bed."

"Oh, Stefan—you can't think like that," Mom tells him. "These things happen."

"But why to *us*?" Dad yells. I hear a thud. I think he's thrown a book or something. It's rare for Dad to get so angry. He's my comedian—the one who makes me laugh. I hate that he feels like this. I don't cry often, but I can't help it now. I lie there, crying into my pillow.

I stay in bed for two more weeks. Nav texts, and so does Ellie, but I don't feel like replying.

Nav is persistent, but I don't answer. I feel too low.

Then I get this message from him: Coming over—don't move!

Before I can tell Mom I don't want any visitors, I hear the bell ring, followed by heavy footsteps running up the stairs.

"Hi," he says, sitting down in the window chair. I am in bed, slightly propped up.

"Hi," I say back.

There's an awkward silence. "So, I think I saw that girl," he tells me, "looking out of the window across the street."

"Really?" I ask. I immediately feel guilty since I've kind of stopped thinking about her. I haven't been well enough to look out.

"Anyway, I've just seen the couple go out," he says. "So I thought you might like to try again. You know, go and knock on the door."

"I'm not up to it, am I?" I huff.

"I can see that," he says. "Well, when you are, we can try again. Dr. Nav thinks you should start building up your stamina again, taking it gradually."

I am not in the mood for his cajoling. "Dr. Nav should stop sticking his nose into my business."

He looks at me, his face dropping. "I'm sorry this happened," he says. "I can't believe you've ended up like this after just one night out."

"I should never have gone," I say angrily. "I certainly shouldn't have stayed afterward."

"It was a mistake," he says, nodding.

"But you encouraged me!"

His eyes are wide. "Because it was what you wanted. It was your decision. It's not fair for you to blame me."

"Well, I do!"

I'm not sure why I'm saying that. I don't really blame him—but he's making me angry. He thinks he knows it all—he made me feel that if I stayed for the party, I'd be okay. And now he's walking in here, uninvited, talking as if it's no big deal.

"Why?" Nav looks really hurt now, but I can't seem to get past my anger.

"You made me believe! All this 'come downstairs, come out in the garden, see how much progress you're making, you'll soon be back at school...' You gave me hope, Nav. And it was a waste of time."

"Sorry I bothered," he mutters. "I thought you liked being with me. I thought we were friends."

"I've got friends, Nav. I don't need you."

He stares at me, clearly shocked. I have shocked myself, too. I should take it back; I should say sorry. But Nav turns and walks out. I hear his feet thud on the stairs and then the front door closing.

"Everything okay?" Mom says, putting her head around my door.

"I didn't feel like seeing anyone. You shouldn't have let him up here," I tell her, switching off the bedside lamp.

"What happened?" Mom sits on the edge of the bed in the dark, but my head is spinning, and I just want to close my eyes and pretend all this isn't happening.

"I need to sleep, Mom. I don't want to talk about it."

"Later then," she says, but I have no intention of talking about it at all.

True to my stubborn word, I still won't talk about Nav the next day, no matter how much Mom presses me.

"I talked to Devi. She says Nav is very upset. What's going on?"

"Leave it, Mom," I tell her.

Eventually she sits back and sighs. "Kasia," she says, "you seem very low, and you're so isolated. I know you have Ellie, but she's busy now studying. I think you need some support. How about looking online for a support group?"

"I looked once and it was full of middle-aged people who've been sick for longer than I've been alive," I remind her.

"But I contacted an ME charity, and they told me there's a Facebook group for teenagers."

"I'm not going to be cheered up by talking to other people who are as miserable as I am, Mom," I protest. "What's the point?"

"You may feel less alone," says Mom. "I'm worried about you."

"I don't want you to worry," I tell her.

"Then you'll have a look, just to keep me happy?" she pleads.

So I look. Although I know there are lots of teenagers with ME, I haven't actually met any. And I'm surprised to find Mom is right. I sign up to the group but have to wait for "approval" before I can see the posts.

The following day I am notified I can access the closed group. I start reading the posts.

There's Dina, who is my age and has been sick for four years. She can cope with half days at school, but is finding it very hard. "People still think I'm faking it, after all this time!" she writes. "They don't understand why I get to go home early. They wouldn't be jealous if they knew how sick I felt and how frustrating it is not to be able to stay at school all day."

Then there's Ariana, who's been confined to bed for two years, yet is able to look at a screen for short bursts. She uses a phone—she doesn't have the strength to hold a tablet—and only uses it for the support group. She is desperate for help, and her mom keeps phoning hospitals and doctors and organizations, but there's no simple cure.

Some people have been offered cognitive behavioral therapy (CBT) and physiotherapy, and something called the Lightning Process. Others have tried alternative therapies, like acupuncture and healing. With all these things, there are some people saying they helped—but also some who feel worse after trying them.

A girl called Mimi has posted a poem she's written about having ME. It's sad but also funny and makes me laugh. I "like" it and comment that I enjoy writing, too, but mostly stories and I'm not well enough to write anything at the moment.

Later I see she's replied, asking me if I'm new to the group and encouraging me to try poetry since it's shorter. She asks me if I like reading, too, and recommends a book.

Although it's depressing to read about people like Ariana,

I am happy to have found people who understand exactly what it's like—especially Mimi.

A few days later I am a little better. On my way back from the bathroom, I go to the window and briefly glance out. I see Nav walking back from the store with a bag of groceries. The good grandson, shopping for his Nani. Bitterness fills my mouth, sour as lemons. I am so full of anger still, and somehow it is all directed at Nav. He doesn't even glance up as he goes back inside.

I lie half listening to a local music station online. The news comes on—and I'm not really paying attention until the words "attempted abduction" catch my ear. Then I start listening closely because the case they're speaking about happened near here. A man started talking to a sixteen-year-old girl who was walking home from school. He asked her the time and then started talking, asking if she knew where he could buy cigarettes. As they turned the corner the man got out a key and opened a parked car and tried to push the girl into it. She struggled and luckily managed to poke him in the eye and run off.

I think back to the night when I saw what looked like a woman being abducted. Could there be a connection? The car described was a different color, and this attack happened in broad daylight, but is it too much of a coincidence? I wish the police had reported back on whether they'd found out anything.

I get up and look out of the window. The girl across the street isn't there. I haven't been looking as much but I haven't seen her for a long time. Nav said he saw her, so she's still in the house. I wonder again if she is being kept prisoner. But she can't really be Farah, can she—that girl from the missing persons website?

19

It's a few more days before I feel well enough to get out of bed and move around regularly. One day I hear the sound of the lawn mower, and I walk to the back bedroom and look out. The yard next door is looking so much better now. Nav has dug up a lot of the old half-dead shrubs and planted new ones, and more are beginning to flower. He definitely has an eye for color. He is mowing in straight lines today, and I feel strangely disappointed. Is it because I upset him? I feel a plum-sized bulge of guilt in my throat. He didn't deserve the way I spoke to him. I text him:

So sorry about what I said.

I look out and see him pull his phone from his pants pocket. I wait expectantly for him to text back or even to look up in the window, but he puts the phone back in his pocket and continues mowing. I realize I should apologize in person, but I'm not in the mood today. Also, deep down, I think I'm scared he may not accept my apology. He'd have every right not to—after what I said. I miss him.

On the first day of the new semester, I hear Mrs. G.'s front door open and close, and Devi's voice calling, "Good luck!" I get out of bed and pull the curtain aside to see Nav in school uniform walking down the road. His walk is bouncy, as if he's really looking forward to it. I wish so much that I was going, too. Right now, I can't imagine that will ever happen.

That afternoon, the doorbell rings, and a part of me almost hopes it's Nav—but it's Ellie who runs up the stairs and into my room. It's great to see her, and though I'm still really down, I feel my spirits lift slightly.

"Hi, chick," she says, bouncing down on to my bed and sending me jerking up as if I'm on a trampoline. "I've got news for you."

"What news?" I ask half-heartedly.

She leans forward and smiles. "You're not going to believe this, Kasia!"

"Spit it out then."

"Josh—he came up to me today. He asked me about you!"

"What?" I sit up. Now this really *is* news. "When? How come? What did he say?"

"He asked how you are, whether I still see you, when you're coming back to school. He was happy when I said you were getting better. I didn't tell him you got worse after the concert."

"It's weird that he's asking now, after all this time!" I say. "I thought he'd forgotten I exist. Maybe he saw me there."

"You still like him, right?" Ellie asks. "Do you want me to tell him you're interested?"

I reel back in horror. "Don't you dare!"

"Okay—calm down. I was only offering!"

I feel myself blush. "I like him, Ellie. Okay? But I saw him with a girl at the concert. I thought they were together."

"Who? Was it Chloe? Nah, they're just friends," says Ellie.

New motivation tingles inside me like fizzy lemonade. "I'm going to pace myself. I'll set targets for myself and build up gradually, and be extra careful about not overdoing it. I'm going to get better and I'm going to tell him exactly how I feel—I won't be shy this time. And I'm going to get back to school, too."

Ellie smiles again. "Good for you."

We talk for a little longer, and then Ellie gets up to go. She turns to me before she leaves. "Oh, Kasia, have you seen anything of that unusual girl at the window you told me about? I keep forgetting to ask you."

"I haven't been well enough to look out much, so no," I tell her. "But what I said about her being that girl on the website—it's strange, isn't it? The woman was probably telling the truth—the girl's eighteen, but looks young for her age and is there helping with the baby."

"Really?" Ellie asks. "You were so suspicious before."

I shrug. "To be honest, I don't know what to think."

After Ellie's gone, I sit by the window, trying to figure out how long it has been since I saw the girl. Then suddenly—as if she's reading my thoughts—she's there. I stare at her. She has the same sad, staring expression as before. I want to take a photo, but my phone's on the bed and I don't want to take my eyes off her. So, I lift my hand and wave. She is watching me—I'm sure. Her hand appears, pressed flat against the window and then released. Then she waves at me. It's the briefest movement, but it's definitely a wave.

So many days I have not dared to look out and, when I have had the courage, there is nothing to see. But today, when I have so little hope, I look and I find what I think is only in my dreams—I find the girl, the girl in the window across the street. Kasia. She is looking back at me. She sees me—and all at once I exist. If she can see me, then I am real. She waves at me, and I am the bravest I have been—I wave back.

I do not dare to stay. The baby cries, and I have to go. Now I think, why did I not do more? Why didn't I try to communicate somehow? Maybe she wouldn't have understood—but maybe she would.

Who knows when I will see her again? Why did I not mouth, Help me*?*

20

True to my word, I start trying to build up my stamina again. I've been pacing myself, restricting my activities and building up very gradually. I've been using Nav's book, which has given me lots of ideas. I rest it on the bed when I'm reading it, like he suggested—though I would never tell him that! I don't know if it's because of the book, or if I was just ready to start again, but I am definitely making progress.

One of the things I've been doing is walking up and down the street, increasing by just a few steps a day. Now I'm actually sitting in the café down the street, five minutes away from home, telling Ellie all about it.

It was Ellie's idea to meet at the café, and it feels amazing—I haven't done anything like this for so long! Ellie stirs her milkshake with a straw and then looks me right in the eye. "Don't kill me, Kasia," she says.

"Why would I kill you?"

"I did something." She hesitates.

"Something?"

"I talked to Josh again."

"What? He spoke to you again, about me?"

"No—this time I spoke to him. He was on his own, standing near the lockers. It seemed like a good opportunity. I couldn't resist!"

"And what happened?" Her sheepish expression is making me nervous. "Are you going to tell me he's asked *you* out?"

"No, no—of course not! I just... I told him about you—how you like him."

"You didn't!" I am stunned and I feel hot all over.

How could she?

"He likes you," says Ellie. "I could tell when he asked about you before. He gave this sweet little smile when I said your name. I mean it, Kas—I'm not making it up."

"What did you say?" I ask. "What did *he* say?"

"I told him you were well on the road to recovery and that you could walk as far as this café."

"And?"

"It was a good hint, you see—because then he said, 'Do you think she'd like to meet me there?'"

"What?" I exclaim. "He really said that? This had better not be a joke!"

"I mean it, Kasia. I said you'd meet him here tomorrow at four."

"OMG!" I don't know whether to be angry with Ellie or

not. I *told* her not to say anything to Josh, though I'm kind of glad she did. Only—tomorrow, that's so soon. I'm not sure if I'm ready. What if I wake up tomorrow and don't feel up to it? What if he's put off when he finds out how little I can do? Will I have the energy to wash my hair? And what on earth am I going to wear?

Well, Ellie can help with that one. "What am I going to wear?" I ask her.

She smiles, looking relieved—I think she was scared I might hit her.

"So you don't mind? You're not angry?"

"I'll take a rain check on that," I tell her.

"Let's go back to your place and have a look in your closet, see what we can find," she suggests.

I nod.

Back in my bedroom I lie on the bed while Ellie stands in front of my open closet.

"My jeans press on my legs," I tell her. "I wore them for the concert, but they really weren't comfy."

"Maybe leggings then? How about these? And this top's nice? You can wear a pretty scarf. Hey—I remember when you bought this!"

She pulls out a shimmery pink scarf. I remember, too. We were at the local market and Ellie spotted it. I loved it right away. It feels like a lifetime ago. I want to be that me again.

"Great idea!" I tell her. "I can't believe I'm going on a

date with Josh! Are you sure you're not making this all up, Ellie?"

"You're the storyteller, not me," Ellie says, laughing. "But try not to think of it as a date—just meeting up in a café. Take it a little slowly, see how things go."

When I wake next morning, I can feel my glands pressing on my neck, and my jaw aches, too. My legs aren't too bad, though, and my head is clear, so I'm pretty certain it's mostly anxiety. I'm going to do this

I'm actually going to meet Josh. I am tempted to skip my usual routine and stay in bed to preserve my energy for later, but I know that's not smart. I will do everything apart from my walk, since I will walk to the café later.

The day feels so long. I listen to podcasts and an audiobook. I do some work for Judy.

"You look nice," says Mom, when she sees me dressed after lunch.

I wish I'd saved the scarf for later, so it didn't look so obvious that I was making an effort.

"Are you meeting Navin? You made up! I'm so glad..."

"Actually Mom," I interrupt. "I'm just meeting a friend in the café. Someone I haven't seen for a while."

"Well, don't..."

"Stay too long," I finish. "Okay, Mom, I do *know* that. You don't have to tell me."

"There's no need to be so angry, Kasia. I only want the best for you, that's all."

I didn't mean to snap at Mom, and I feel terrible, seeing the hurt look on her face.

"Sorry, Mom, I just want to be treated like I'm normal for once—not some fragile piece of china. I won't stay more than half an hour, I promise."

As I walk down the sidewalk, I wonder whether it is better to be waiting there for him or if that might look too anxious. I don't want to keep him waiting, though.

I am so nervous. In the end I arrive on the dot of four, but Josh isn't here yet. Two minutes go by and I start to panic that he's not coming. And then he walks through the door.

I'm breathing too fast. I try to slow it down. For so long now, I've been a girl who's sick—that has become my identity. It's like I can barely remember the person I used to be—a girl who might meet a boy in a café. Josh is in his school uniform. His long hair suits him, and his eyes are smiling at me even more than his mouth.

"Hiya," he says, sitting down across from me. "Long time no see!"

"Hi," I say. I smile back.

There's an awkward pause. I've got to say something else but...what? I am so relieved when he speaks.

"How's that woman you saved? She okay?"

"Yes." The word comes out much quieter than I expect. I feel myself blushing. How does he know about Mrs. G.? Maybe Ellie told him.

"I had a great-aunt," he tells me. "She died after a stroke. No one found her for three days. I wish she'd had a neighbor like you—to call an ambulance and that. Maybe she'd have been okay."

"That's sad," I say.

I can't think what else to say. I've said four words so far altogether. He'll think I can't talk clearly if I don't manage a full sentence.

"Do you want a drink, a cake or something?" he asks.

"Thanks—a hot chocolate, please."

He grins. "That's what I want, too. Whipped cream on top?"

I nod and wait while he goes to order. I wonder if I should offer to pay.

There's a couple in the corner, but apart from that the café's empty. I'm glad it isn't full of kids from school.

He sits down with the drinks. I sip mine and feel an instant moustache of cream above my lip. How embarrassing! The whipped cream was a mistake—I should have thought. I wipe my mouth quickly with a napkin.

"It's delicious. Thank you," I tell him.

He smiles, but he doesn't say anything else. It's up to me. I'm struggling to think of something to say.

"How's orchestra?" I ask. "I thought the show was great!"

His eyebrows go up. "Were you there?"

Oh my God! He didn't even notice me. I was sure he had! But then he was busy playing in the concert and talking to people afterward—like that Chloe.

"Yeah, I made a big effort to come," I tell him. "I overdid it actually."

I mentally kick myself—why did I bring *that* up?

"I hope you'll be back in the orchestra soon," he says. "We're playing Beethoven's Symphony No. 5 this term."

"Oh, I love that!" I find myself humming it aloud and he grins.

"So you're much better now?" he says. "I mean, you look fine—you look great. I like the scarf."

I feel myself blushing as I nod. "I'm definitely on the mend."

"Will you be back at school in September?"

"I hope so," I say. "That's what I want anyway."

"A friend of my mom's has ME," he tells me. "She's had it for years, so I know a little about it."

"Really?" I'm not sure if this is a good thing or not. It might make him more understanding, but he could also think I might never get better. That's what I worry about. I mean, I know I'm not his girlfriend, but who'd want to go out with someone who's always sick?

"It's good you're getting over it," he says. "It's really a bummer getting something like that."

"It hasn't been easy," I say.

"So what do you do all day at home?" he asks.

"I have a tutor who comes once a week, so I do some schoolwork," I say. "I listen to music, podcasts, and audiobooks, and I sit and look out the window. Now that I'm getting better, I go for short walks, too."

"God, that must be so dull! Are you up to going to see a movie?" he asks.

I meet his eyes. He is actually asking me out—on a date! So many things whirl through my head, but how can I say yes? I can't even cope with TV right now, so how could I sit in the movies? The brightness of the screen, the flashing movements, loud soundtracks—I can already feel a headache coming on at the thought. But if I say no, he might never ask me again.

"What movie?" I ask, playing for time.

"I'll have a look and see what's showing," he says, taking out his phone.

I want to say yes. My heart says yes, but my head is panicking.

Josh looks up at me and frowns. "Are you okay?"

"Yes." I nod emphatically, trying to shut up the inner voices.

He holds out his phone and points to a movie. "This is out next Friday. Have you heard about it? I really want to see it."

"Oh—yes, me, too. I read a review online."

And that's true—I really do want to see it. It would have been an easier decision if he'd said a movie that I knew I'd hate.

"So—next Friday, then? Is it a date?" he asks, smiling.

A date. He actually said the word. Those eyes—they've dazzled me, sent me buzzing, because I hear myself answer with the words I know I shouldn't say.

"Yes, that'd be great."

His smile is worth it, but my head is beginning to throb.

"I have to go now," I tell him. "But this was nice."

"Should I walk you home?" he offers.

"No, that's okay," I say. I would have liked him to, but if Mom sees him, I know she'll pound me with questions I'm not yet ready to answer.

"Can I have your number then?" he asks—and I give it to him. And he gives me his, too. I now have Josh's number in my phone.

I stand up and my legs feel wobbly. I have to hold on to the table for a moment.

"Are you sure I can't walk you home?" he says again.

I take deep breaths, hoping desperately that I'm not going to collapse on the floor, then shake my head. "I stood up too quickly," I tell him. "I'm fine now."

I pull my wallet out of my bag.

"It's okay. Put that away," he says.

"Thanks."

"See you Friday then," he says. "I'll text you."

"Bye, Josh."

We walk in opposite directions, and I can't resist a quick glance back at him. Did all that really happen?

When I get home, the strength drains from me, and I can't face the stairs. I lie on the sofa for a while. "You haven't overdone it, have you, Kasia?" Mom fusses when she finds me later.

"No, I just felt like resting here for a while," I lie.

"Good girl," says Mom.

But I don't know what I'm going to do now. I'm so thrilled that Josh has actually asked me out, but I know the movies are a bad idea. I've said yes, though, so I've got to go.

Ellie comes over right after school next day. I've made it downstairs, and she's cross-legged beside me on the sofa.

"So—tell me all!" she demands. "How did it go with Josh?"

"We're going on a date on Friday—to the movies!" I tell her.

"But you told me you can't even watch TV!"

"I couldn't say no," I say. "But I don't know what to do. I'm not really up to it."

Ellie's smile falters a little. "You can't just do stuff because someone else wants you to, you know."

"I know!" I say. "But it wasn't that easy. He likes me, I can tell, and I do want to go on a date with him."

"But you've gone all gooey over him! Don't let your heart rule your head, or you'll end up in trouble."

"I'm not gooey!" I protest. "I just don't want to mess this up. What do you think I should do? Tell him the truth—that I'm not up to it? I might never hear from him again."

"But he *has* to know, doesn't he?" Ellie says. "If you're going on a date with him, you can't just pretend you're okay."

"I'm getting better all the time," I remind her. "I don't want to blow him off."

"So you're going to go to watch a movie even though you don't feel up to it?"

"Shhh," I say, looking anxiously toward the bedroom door. "I don't want my mom to hear."

She lowers her voice. "You're going to go to watch a movie even though you don't feel up to it and you're not even going to tell your *mom* what you're doing?"

"If I tell her, she won't let me go."

"This sounds like a bad idea, Kasia."

"Thanks! Don't forget you set this all up in the first place!"

"Just be careful, that's all I'm saying," says Ellie. Her voice softens, and she makes me soften, too.

I don't want to fall out with Ellie like I did Nav—I don't know what I'd do without my best friend.

"I will be careful, Els. If the movie is too flashy, I'll just close my eyes and meditate. I'm sure Josh won't notice."

Ellie laughs.

That night I can't sleep. I'm thinking about Josh and worrying about the movies. I can't lie still. I get up and sit by the window, drawing the curtain aside so I can look out. There is a light on in the upstairs room opposite. The curtains are closed, but they must be thin because I can see a silhouette behind them. Is it the girl? I'm sure it must be.

She seems to be just standing there. Maybe the baby has woken up and she is trying to sing him back to sleep. I wish she'd open the curtain and look out. Maybe she would wave to me again.

As I watch I see another silhouette, taller and broader than the girl. I can't be sure, but it could be the woman who lives there. The silhouettes move, blurred. It's like watching a shadow puppet play. The arm of the bigger silhouette suddenly swings around, and the smaller silhouette drops out of view.

I gasp. What just happened? I can't be sure, but it looked as if the woman hit the girl in the head so hard that she fell. Did I really see what I thought I saw? With shadows, it's very hard to tell what's happening.

I go back to bed and lie awake for hours.

The baby cried so much today, and even I could not soothe him. I cannot keep my eyes open. I sneak to my room to lie down, while they eat downstairs. If I don't lie down, I think I will fall. I just want to rest, but I sleep. I did not mean to sleep. I wake with a fright, and Auntie is here, screaming. I jump up so fast. The baby is crying again, and I did not go to him. Lazy, she calls me. Lazy, good for nothing. How dare I lie down? How dare I ignore the baby when he cries!

I feel so angry. "I work hard," I tell her.

"How dare you answer back!" she screams, her mouth opens wide like a lion's as she roars. "You are nothing! So ungrateful! You forget how lucky you are to have a home here. You go to him make him stop crying right now!" she demands. "This must not happen again!"

I rush to the baby. I hug him, rock him until he finally sleeps. I am so tired. Too tired.

When I finally can go to bed, I must sleep very deeply, because suddenly the light is on, and she is yelling again.

"What is wrong with you? Can't you hear him crying? Did you not hear my warning before? You stupid girl!"

I stand quickly, wiping the sleep from my eyes. "I'm so sorry! I didn't hear!"

Her hand is raised, and she shoves me so hard, I hit the wall behind.

I go to the baby, but it takes a long time to soothe him back to sleep. When I return to bed I want to sleep, but I cannot. This time it is me that cries.

21

Friday has taken so long to come around. Every hour has seemed to last two—but now it's really here. I am going on a date—a date with Josh. I'm not feeling great, mostly due to lack of sleep and overexcitement, but I am not too bad. Mom and Dad are going out, too, for their anniversary. I've convinced Mom that I'm well enough to be left on my own, so I don't need to tell any lies about where I'm going. They are going early, and I will be back before them. This is clearly meant to be!

Josh texts to say he'll meet me at the bus stop. I hadn't even thought about how we were going to get to the movies. I haven't been on a bus for months and months. At least the bus stop is close and has seats, and we can get off right outside the theater. I decide I will watch out of the window and go down early, as soon as a bus leaves, so I can be sure of getting a seat at the bus stop. Even if have to sit there an extra ten minutes, it will be worth it.

When the time comes, I head out, crossing the street carefully. Some people are waiting for a different bus, so there are only two free seats, but I get one of them and sigh with relief.

I feel a nudge as someone sits down beside me. I am astonished to see that it's the woman from across the street—the woman from number 48.

She doesn't speak, but I'm sure she recognizes me. I think about what I might have seen last night in the window. The woman is sitting here so casually, and she looks so ordinary. She couldn't have hit the girl, could she? Maybe it was the man—or maybe it simply didn't happen. I want to say something—to ask about the girl. I try to frame sentences in my mind—something I could say to start a conversation.

"Hi," I say awkwardly. She turns in surprise.

"Do you remember me?" I ask. "I live across the street."

She nods and gives a small rather forced half smile. Then she looks at the ground. She obviously doesn't want to talk to me, but I continue talking anyway.

"How's the baby?" I try. "Is your niece still helping you out?"

"The baby's fine—he's growing fast," she tells me. "Getting heavy!" She holds her arms out as if carrying a heavy weight and laughs. "And my niece is a great help—I'm lucky to have her."

Now she seems friendly, though I'm sure it's an act. It's

so hard to tell. I try to think what else I can say. Do I dare ask again if the girl would like to meet up?

At that moment a bus pulls up, and the woman gives me a nod as she stands. Then she turns away and steps on to the bus.

"Hiya! You look like you're in a dream!"

I jolt as Josh sits down beside me in the spot the woman has vacated.

"You okay?" he asks.

"Yeah." I smile at him, and his eyes meet mine. They sparkle in a way that makes my heart flutter. Maybe Ellie's right—I am going gooey.

He looks at his watch. Was I staring back too hard? "Bus shouldn't be long," he says.

I'm glad, because I'm finding the hard bench uncomfortable. It's hurting the back of my legs, and I could really do with my cushion, but it would have been too embarrassing to bring it with me.

When the bus comes, the seats are at least more comfortable, but I had forgotten how bumpy a bus can be. The way the bus swings around corners and stops abruptly at red lights makes me ache and feel slightly queasy. I cling on tight to the pole beside me, while trying to look relaxed and carefree.

"You sure you're okay?" he asks.

"Yeah." I need to change the subject. "How's school?" I try.

"S'all right," he says. "So much homework, though—it's

doing me in. I'm tired—I can imagine what it's like for you, now!"

"It's not quite the same," I reply, feeling a flash of irritation. "It's not like normal tiredness." I realize I sounded a little abrupt. I didn't mean to snap at him. "I'm sure all that studying must be really hard, though," I add.

"Yes! I'll be so glad when the exams are over. Do you know Ricky and Raj?"

I shake my head. "What about them?"

"Oh—it's nothing. Not really interesting if you don't know them."

I'm not sure what else to say. I feel like we're struggling for conversation. Maybe once we get off the bus it will be easier.

"Have you seen any other good movies lately?" I ask.

"Not really," he says. "The last movie I saw wasn't great. Chloe thought it was okay, but..."

"Chloe?" I can't help commenting. "Is she your ex or something?"

"No—we're friends," he answers.

I feel myself relax a little. We sit silently, and I think maybe this is okay—to be relaxed together and not feel we have to talk all the time.

At last we reach the theater.

The movie isn't bad, though it's a little violent, and it reminds me of what I saw last night across the street. I wonder again what really happened, and I think about the woman at the bus stop—was she being friendly, or was she just pretending in order to shut me up? Then I feel Josh's fingers reaching for mine. He's holding my hand. His hand is soft and warm and gentle.

But although I'm caught up in the movie and loving the feel of Josh's hand in mine, the action scenes are increasing and there are too many flashes and bangs. I start to feel unwell.

"Going to the bathroom," I whisper, pulling my hand from his clasp.

The dark of the stairs in contrast to the brightness of the screen makes my head spin and I'm relieved to be out in the lobby. When I reach the bathrooms, I splash my face with water, but I don't feel any better. The glands in my neck are pulsing painfully, my head's thumping, and I feel weak and dizzy. I realize I won't be able to go back in. I can't face it. What is Josh going to think?

I stumble back out into the lobby and sit down on the floor, leaning against the wall. I am not sure how much time passes before Josh appears, looking worried.

"There you are! I thought you were taking a long time. What's wrong?"

"I'm sorry, Josh." Tears start sliding feebly down my face. "I just don't feel all that great. I'll probably be okay in a minute."

"There's only half an hour to go," he says. "Come and watch the end, and then I'll take you home. It's only sitting down."

I shake my head. "I can't. You go back in if you want. I'll just stay here."

"Really?"

He looks uncertain, but he's edging back toward the door to the theater. I feel another wave of irritation that he would do this instead of looking after me. But I brought this on myself. I should never have agreed to come.

"I don't think there'll be a bus for half an hour, anyway," he says.

When I look up, I realize that I can't wait even that long.

"Josh, actually, I need to go home now. And I don't feel up to getting the bus."

"What? Do you want to call your mom to come and get you then? I don't have money for a cab."

Tears are streaming down my face now. I feel such a fool. "My mom doesn't know I'm here."

He raises his eyebrows. "Why not? Doesn't she like you dating?"

I don't answer.

"Where does she think you are?" he asks.

"At home."

"So, what do you want to do?" he asks.

I'm panicked. I can't think. "Ellie's house isn't far from here," I tell him, "Crown Street. If I can make it there, maybe she'll lend me the money for a cab."

I'm not actually sure I can even manage the short walk to Ellie's, but I don't want to admit that.

"Sure—I know Crown Street. Here—hold my hand," he says, helping me up.

We make it to Ellie's, and she and her mom fuss over me. Her mom kindly offers to drive me home. I am so grateful. Josh says he hopes I feel better soon, but he doesn't say anything about texting me or seeing me again.

Back at home, I can't face the stairs. I lie on the sofa, and suddenly I'm crying, and I can't stop. I've messed it up with Josh. I've messed it up completely. It was too soon—I should have waited until I was much better.

And now I've lost him. Why would he want to date a girl who can't even sit through a movie without feeling sick? I feel so pathetic, so stupid. I just about make it up to bed before Mom and Dad get back.

I have three days where I'm barely able to move. "Very strange," says Mom, "this sudden relapse out of nowhere. And when you'd been doing so well."

Josh doesn't text. I feel angry. Maybe he doesn't want to go out with me anymore, but to not even check on how I'm doing isn't nice. I'm sure he'll call.

Three more days go by, and I am still in bed. I'm feeling

worse. The whole trip to the movies was too much—the bus ride, the strobe-like action of the movie, the walk back to Ellie's. I can't stand the light now and need the curtains closed all the time or my head starts pounding. I don't even feel like I can sit up. I feel so low—as if I have fallen down a deep, deep well. I am stuck in the dark at the bottom and I can't move. Someone found me and I thought I was going to be rescued, but all they have done is lowered a tube to give me water. I am being kept alive, but no one knows how to get me out. What kind of life is this?

I thought I could fight this illness and beat it, but I can't. It always wins. Maybe I am never going to get back to school, never going to be able to have a relationship. If this is my life now, then what's the point? I am not sure if I want to live like this.

Gradually over the next few days I can tolerate light and sit up for a while. After a few more days, I don't feel able to get out of bed, but I am able to go online for short spurts. I try to distract myself with the Facebook support group. I write about how depressed I feel about my life, but when I read it back it sounds like I am wallowing in self-pity, and I delete it all—every word.

But later, I try again. I write about what happened with Josh in more of a storytelling style, and when I read it back, I'm happy with it. I've managed to laugh at myself and my lovesick stupidity, which is something. I didn't name him, of course—even though it's a closed group, I wouldn't want anyone knowing all the details.

I decide to post it on the website, but when I check after half an hour, no one has "liked" it or commented on it, and I feel a wave of disappointment. Maybe they'd rather compare symptoms than talk about relationships.

But later on I check again and I have three "likes" and two comments. Dina says, "Don't be so hard on yourself. You liked him, so it makes sense that you really wanted to go. I've never had a date with a boy. The only time one asked me, I had to cancel three times, and then he gave up, believing I was giving him the brush-off—even though I tried so hard to explain it was because I wasn't well. I hate letting people down all the time. It is so hard to have a boyfriend when you are like this."

Mimi says, "Thank you for cheering me up, Kasia! I've been having such a bad day, and you wrote this in such a funny way, it made me laugh and laugh. I can see what a good writer you are!"

I am cheered by these replies, but still sad, too. I messed up my one chance, and I can't stand it. Josh hasn't texted me at all, and I'm not sure whether I should text him after what happened.

Ellie texts me a few times. I tell her not to come over since I really can't face anyone—but she turns up anyway.

"Are you angry with me?" she asks, flopping down in the chair by my bed. "I never meant for this to happen. I was only trying to help."

"I know, Ells," I assure her. "Of course I don't blame you. I should have been honest with Josh about the movie. We could have done something else instead."

"So when do you think you'll see him again?"

I shake my head. "I won't. He hasn't texted or anything."

"No way!" says Ellie. "He seems so nice!"

"I can't really blame him," I say, sighing. "I know it's hard for people to understand because I look okay—they can't tell how sick I feel."

"You still want to see him?" Ellie asks.

I shrug. "It doesn't matter, does it? He clearly doesn't want to see me. I think it's over, Els." Tears start to roll down my cheeks, and I can't stop them. "I want to feel special and close to someone and loved, you know? And I want to go to school. I want a normal life."

"Yes, I know," says Ellie, giving me a gentle hug. "But maybe forget about him for a while. Let's just try and get you better first."

22

Even though nothing has really changed, Ellie's words have cheered me up, and so have the responses on the Facebook group. Today I feel like sitting and looking out of the window for the first time in days. There is nothing to see at the house across the street. The curtains upstairs are closed. I turn to the bus stop and watch the people for a while. I think about the woman from 48 sitting next to me there and wonder what she's doing today.

I walk to my parents' bedroom so I can look out the back. I am kind of hoping Nav will be there, in the garden next door—and he is. He's planting something in a flower bed. The garden is looking beautiful now, in the sunshine. It's full of flowers.

Maybe today I'll try to go downstairs. I'd love to sit outside with Nav, watch him gardening, and have us talk like we used to. Why am I so stupid? Why was I so mean to him? I wonder whether I should try texting him again.

Then I see that Mrs. Gayatri is sitting out there—on the chair that I used to use. I'm happy for her, glad she feels well enough—but I'm disappointed, too. Nav has company already.

I go back to bed instead. I will forget about boys and concentrate on my studying. I open a file and try to write answers to some history questions. I have to do enough work so that they will let me stay with my classmates.

When Judy comes, she is impressed with the work I've done.

"I want to get back to school in September—even part-time or something," I tell her.

I see the immediate doubt in Judy's frown. "Kasia, I think you have to be realistic about it. I also hope you'll get back to school part-time in September, but I still believe you'll have to repeat tenth grade and cut the number of classes you're taking, too."

I can't answer. I can't speak. This is not what I want to hear.

"Kasia?"

I have to prove her wrong. I must.

I am getting better and better, and I'm feeling more positive, too. I begin to go downstairs and move around the house again, and it's not too long before I decide to go out for my first walk in a long time. I stand on the front doorstep and let the sunshine warm my face. I breathe in the fresh air. I look across the street at number 48. I wonder about ringing the bell again. It's such a beautiful day—warm and sunny but not too hot—even if she's a few years old than me, maybe I could convince the shy girl to come out for a short walk—to the café perhaps. It's so long since I've seen her—but she did wave to me that once.

I decide to take the risk. I ring the bell. The woman comes to the door. She looks at me suspiciously.

"I've just come to ask after your niece," I tell her. "It's such a nice day—I wondered if she'd like to come to the café with me. She could bring the baby, too."

"My niece is fine. She is busy and not in need of company, as I told you before," the woman says. Then, as if worried she has spoken too sharply, she adds, "It is kind of you to ask, though."

"Doesn't she ever want to come outside?" I press.

"Of course she does. But not today." And she closes the door abruptly.

There's nothing more I can do.

Over the next few weeks I focus on increasing my walking and studying, determined to go back to school in September. The first time I manage a fifteen-minute walk, I feel amazing! It's the most I've walked in nearly a year—a whole year. I am managing more studying, too.

One day I see Mrs. G., who is taking out a bag for recycling. We are very happy to see each other.

"Off anywhere nice?" she asks.

"Just up and down the street. I'm trying to build up my steps," I tell her.

"Why don't you go to the park?" Mrs. Gayatri suggests. "You know—the one on Alwyn Road? Wouldn't that be nicer than walking up and down the street?"

"That's a good idea," I say, nodding. "I couldn't get that far before, but I think I could now. It would be a change of scene. I haven't been there for years."

"I haven't been there for many years, either," says Mrs. G. "I used to push Devi there in her stroller."

The park is a little more than ten minutes away, but I make it there—through the park gate and on to a bench. I hope I will be okay to walk back again. Sitting there, I feel a sense of calm as I look across the grass to the pond, watching the gently rippling water, the trees rustling. I can hear the road, but it is a gentle hum in the distance—the birdsong of the park fills the air. Two ducks glide across the water, hopeful for food. I feel a tiny thrill inside to have walked this far. Mrs. G. is right—it's so much nicer than the street.

I sit breathing calmly and enjoying just being here, watching the passersby. There's a man pushing a stroller. Then a girl comes. She's pushing a stroller, too. She approaches the pond and pulls out a bag of bread crusts. The ducks change direction, instantly heading toward her. The girl reaches into the bag of bread. There's a sign up saying PLEASE DON'T FEED BREAD TO

THE DUCKS, but she doesn't seem to have noticed. I wonder if I ought to say something, but I don't want to interfere.

She has long dark hair swept back in an untidy ponytail. She's wearing a thin top and a skirt that doesn't seem to fit her correctly. There's something familiar about her. My heart skips a beat as I catch sight of her face. It can't be...can it? She's the girl I've seen in the window—the girl from number 48. But how can it be her? The gray stroller is familiar—it's like the one I've seen the woman from 48 pushing a couple of times. It must be her. I watch intently as she feeds the ducks, talking to the baby. It is so weird to see her outside—in the park, after all this time. She looks okay—perfectly normal. I've had all these crazy thoughts about her and now here she is, at the park, looking fine. I want to speak to her. I hope she might turn this way and see me. Maybe she'll recognize me, too. But she's looking only at the baby and the ducks. She gives the baby a crust, and I see his arm try to throw but the bread lands next to the stroller. The girl bends to pick it up and throws it herself.

I stand up and meander toward her, trying to look as if I'm just wandering over to take a look at the pond. I stand a few feet away. Now that I'm up close, I can see that she's definitely not Farah, the girl from the missing persons website. Her face is a similar shape, but her eyes and mouth are different.

The baby turns and looks at me with curious eyes. "Hi," I say to the girl. "Cute baby."

The girl tenses. She keeps looking straight ahead at the pond, clutching the bag of bread crusts tightly as if she thinks I want to steal them. It was a friendly comment, but I feel like she is radiating fear. Something must be very wrong for her to react this way.

The baby giggles at me. "Bababa," he says, pointing at the ducks.

"Ducks?" I say to him. "You like feeding the ducks?" He grins.

The girl takes another crust from the bag and throws it. She's still acting as if I'm not there.

"Do you recognize me?" I ask gently. "I've seen you in the window. I live across the street. I've never seen you outside before. I wondered if you were okay? I'm not being nosy or anything. I just... Are you okay?"

I'm babbling. She isn't answering.

"Do you speak English?" I ask, suddenly wondering if she's understood a word I said.

She grabs the handles of the stroller and walks quickly away toward the gate.

"Sorry," I call after her. "I didn't mean to upset you. I was only..." But she's through the gate and gone before I can finish my sentence.

"See—I am kind. I will let you go out. Don't speak to anyone." That's what she told me today. It is so long since I've been anywhere—I can barely believe what she says.

She told me the way to the park, and to come right back. I am happy to be alone here with the baby and the birds—to enjoy the air that smells of pine cones and to feel the sun on my back. If I speak, bad things will happen.

Then the girl approaches. What does she want? Who is she? Then I realize I know this girl. She is Kasia from across the street. Her voice is kind and gentle. I want to talk—to tell her—but I don't have the words. And I am too scared. I want her to go, to leave me alone. But she keeps talking and I can't understand much she says.

I must leave before I find my words because they might come out—and that is dangerous, too dangerous. I walk quickly, the bag of bread still in my hand.

Kasia can't see me now. The hunger gnaws at my stomach.

I stand by a tree. There is no one in sight. The motion of walking has sent the baby to sleep. I pull a crust from the bag, hard and rough, with a tinge of blue. It is repulsive, but I have not eaten since yesterday, and then just scraps. The bread still smells of bread. My stomach aches for it. I stuff it into my mouth. Then more, one crust after another until it's gone. Then I go back to the house.

23

When I get home, I sit in my room by the window, wondering why the girl hurried off so quickly. Maybe I shouldn't have spoken to her. I think I frightened her with all my questions.

I feel so tired now, but I'm glad I managed the walk to the park. I'll go there tomorrow, as long as I feel up to it. Maybe the girl will be there again—or maybe she'll look out of the window tonight.

When Judy comes in the afternoon, she's impressed by the amount of work I've done. But when she tries to teach me, I can't concentrate at all.

"Kasia, if you continue like this, I worry that you won't take all your classes next year. I know how much you want to achieve that, but your health has to come first. You shouldn't overstretch yourself."

I bite my lip. "Maybe you're right and that's not realistic."

Judy's face lights up. "Finally!"

"Maybe I could just do six—or seven."

"I'll tell you what: Taking fewer classes and doing them a year later will not hold you back in life."

"You might be right," I grudgingly admit.

"You need to listen to your body and pace yourself. You can study at any time in your life—you don't have to stick to some government schedule. You have to do what's right for you."

It's evening but still light when I glance out of the window and suddenly she's there—the girl in the window opposite. She's looking straight at me. Does she recognize me from the park? I hope so. Maybe she doesn't understand English—maybe that's why she seemed so scared earlier, she didn't realize I was the girl who'd waved to her.

She's still staring at me. I'm sure she realizes it was me. How can I tell her I just want to know if she's okay? If she needs help, I want to help her.

I try to mouth the words "Are you okay?" But then she's gone.

A few days later I make it back to the park. The sun is bright again, smiling down on me warmly, and I feel positive. I believe I will get better. One day my life will get back to normal, and this illness will be something I simply look back on as a bad memory.

The park is busier today than when I came last. The warmer weather has brought more people out of the shadows. It is particularly popular with people who have babies. I look out hopefully for the girl with the stroller, but I don't see her.

My phone vibrates. There's a message from Marek.

I open it eagerly.

"Guess where I am?" he asks.

My heart thuds. Has he come back? Is he at home? "Where?"

The next message is a photo. It's a front door. It looks vaguely familiar, but it isn't ours.

Then another photo—a smiling face. This I do recognize. It's my Aunt Maria in Poland.

"Lodz!" I reply.

"Yes—I'm home," he tells me.

"This is home—HERE," I message. "Not Poland."

"It feels like home," he responds. "At least I am with family who welcome me with open arms. It's nice to see our cousins. I'm going to stay a while and work with Uncle Andrzej."

"Dad is not going to be happy," I respond.

"Dad is never happy," Marek replies.

And I'm right. Dad is mortified. He switches immediately into overdramatic mode.

"It's a complete humiliation," he tells Mom, thumping

the table so hard that a teaspoon jumps in the air. "I told them so many times how much better life is here—the opportunities there are for our children. Now my good-for-nothing son goes crawling back begging for work in your brother's bakery—sweeping the floor! It's a disgrace! How they'll be laughing."

"He's a little lost, our Marek," says Mom, a wistful look in her eyes. "He will find his way in time."

"Lost! After all the guidance we have given him!"

I cannot stand to hear them arguing, so I go to lie down on my bed.

As I lie staring at the ceiling, a memory floats into my head. It's a hot day, years ago. We are lying on the grass side by side in the park, the one on Alwyn Road.

Mom is sitting on a bench somewhere near, talking with a friend.

"What do you want to do when you grow up?" I ask Marek.

"I don't know," he says.

"A soccer player?" I ask.

"I love soccer, but I'm not good enough," he tells me. "What about you, Kas? You're clever. You could do anything."

"An author, or a musician, or a doctor, or a scientist, maybe," I reply.

"Wow! That's a lot of ideas! Whatever you do, you must use that amazing brain of yours."

"You have a brain, too," I say. "There are so many different jobs—I don't know how anyone decides what to do."

"You don't have to decide yet," he tells me. "We don't have to decide for years and years and years. There's plenty of time."

I am watching TV with the baby. It is—which is very good for learning English. I feel like a normal person, sitting on sofa. I have never sat here before. Watching TV—this is my reward—because I work hard. She says it's good for the baby to watch.

She says, "See, you are good and things are better for you. You take the baby to the park and now watch TV. You have a good life, we are kind to you. Yes?"

I nod. I hope I am allowed to go the park again soon.

My stomach rumbles. On TV, some teddy bears are eating cake.

24

Today in the park I am stunned to see the girl right away. There she is by the pond again, whispering affectionately to the baby in the stroller, who stares up at her with his big, round eyes. I stop still, staring, my heart beating fast. This feels so important. I don't want to frighten her, but I am determined to speak to her again—and this time I don't want her to run away.

She hasn't seen me yet. I walk slowly closer until I see her shoulders tense. She glances at me.

"Please don't run off," I say to her. "I don't want to scare you. I only want to talk. I want to know that you are okay."

She shuffles nervously, and I think she is going to leave.

I need to keep talking to her. I need to make her stay.

"I hardly ever see you outside the house," I continue. "You're always inside."

"You also," she whispers, glancing up at me and then back toward the pond.

My heart is racing. She's speaking to me—she *does* understand, though she has a strong accent.

"Yes, I've been sick," I tell her. "And you? Is it the same for you? Are you sick?"

"Sick?" she repeats as if unsure what it means.

"Ill, not well, feeling bad," I try.

She shakes her head. "I not sick," she says.

"So why don't you go outside?" I ask.

"I am here—outside," she says, still barely audible, a puzzled look on her face.

"But you hardly ever come out, do you?"

"Yes, many days inside," she says, nodding. "Lots of work."

"Schoolwork?" I ask.

She shakes her head. "No school for me. Baby, house—lots of work. You not go school," she comments. "You home many times, too."

"I'm not well enough to go to school," I tell her. "How old are you?"

She doesn't answer. "What's your name?"

She's gone quiet, and I'm not sure what to say. I want to ask her about the woman dragged into the car, whether she saw—but she's not answering questions about her name or her age, so I don't want to press her.

"Are you really okay? Do you need help?" I ask.

"Help? How you help? You want care for this baby?"

I have a sudden thought. "Is he yours? Is that why you're not at school?"

"My baby? No! But I care for him much."

"You shouldn't have to care for him all the time, though," I tell her. "You should get days off. Are you happy?"

I see her eyes darken for a moment. She isn't. I'm sure she isn't. Her whole posture, her bent shoulders, her scared eyes say she's not.

"Happy?" She shrugs. "My life not so bad. I love baby."

"He's really cute." I smile. She nods.

"Now I must go."

I'm frustrated. I'm sure she's not telling me everything.

"Can you meet me here again?" I ask her. "I just want to be your friend."

"Friend is good." She gives me the briefest smile back.

"Tomorrow?" I ask. "Can you come tomorrow?"

She shakes her head.

"Friday?"

"I try," she says, and she walks quickly away.

I am afraid.

I spoke to the girl—to Kasia. She spoke to me. She is kind, but I broke the rule. Speak to no one. Will they know? Do they have eyes everywhere? Do they watch? Will I be punished?

When I get back from the park, I hear a voice. There is someone here. Someone different. It's a girl, and she's crying. He calls me and I run upstairs. I must always run to him when he calls.

"That girl in there," he barks, "she is sick. You will nurse her. Make sure she takes this medicine. You understand?"

I nod meekly. "Does she need food?" I dare to ask.

His glare makes me instantly regret my words. "You think I'm an idiot? You think I will give you food for her so that you can eat it all? Your aunt will see to her food. You give her water and medicine and tell Auntie if she gets any worse. She must get better quickly and return to work. I am losing money."

Then he looks at me, and I don't like it. It is as if he can see through my clothes, and it makes me shudder inside.

"You could always be her replacement," he says, his voice low and full of threat. "If I had my way you would be there already, but your auntie likes you. She says you are good with the baby. She wants you here to work in the house. But if that girl does not recover soon, I will have it my way. Don't you forget that."

He's gone. I am not stupid. I know what he means. I know what work this girl does. My life is bad, but not like that.

I cautiously open the door. She is older than me by three or four years. She lies sobbing on a mattress the same as mine. There is no sheet, no cover. She wears only shorts and a T-shirt. Her long matchstick legs have clear bruises. She is shaking, I think with cold—but as I get closer I can feel the heat coming from her. She has a fever, not chill.

I speak my own tongue to her, but she does not respond.

She may be too sick or maybe she doesn't understand.

"I have medicine for you," I tell her. "A tablet to take with water. You must take it and you will feel better."

"For what?" I hear her whisper. She does speak my tongue after all.

I don't have the answer to this. "You want to die?" I ask.

"I care not if I live or die," she says.

"If you live there can be hope for something better to happen. If you die there is no chance, no hope," I reply.

"Something better. You think there is something better? There is not. There is nothing. This is it."

Her voice is quiet but bitter, desolate. She makes me afraid. I cannot lose hope like this girl has. I need to believe in the better. I must.

She slowly sits up and takes the tablet with a sip of water.

Then she turns away from me and lies back down.

She is here for four days, but she does not speak to me again. Then her fever has gone. Then so has she.

The other girl recovered but now I have her fever. I realize they brought her here to protect the other girls from catching it. They wanted me to tend to her so they didn't catch it themselves. I know now how bad the girl felt.

Auntie tries to insist that I do my chores, but she sees that I cannot. She says since I am sick, she will be kind and let me rest. She gives me the tablet and the water, but no food. She says best not to eat if I am sick. But my body has no strength to fight this illness—I am so weak from lack of food, I think I will almost certainly die.

I wish I'd told the girl, Kasia, my name so someone knows I was a person once—a person with a name, someone who lived.

I am too hot and then so cold I shake—and then too hot again. I dream of scraps—of moldy bread meant for birds. I cannot even dream of decent food now. It is so long since I had some.

She keeps me away from the baby—she does not want him to catch this fever. He is my warmth, my consolation, and I miss him. I know he cries for me, and she cannot soothe him.

25

Next time Ellie comes to visit, I tell her all about meeting the girl in the park.

"So, what the woman told you could be true," she says when I finish.

I nod. "The girl does go out, and she is looking after the baby, but she didn't answer when I asked how old she is. No way does she look eighteen, and she seemed scared about something. I've still got a bad feeling about it."

"Maybe I could come with you at the weekend?" Ellie suggests. "See if she's there?"

"Yes, please!" I tell her.

I go to the park on Friday and I sit on the bench for a long while, but the girl doesn't come. I watch from the window in the evening, but I don't see her then, either. Ellie comes with me on Saturday, but there is still no sign of her. Ellie seems as disappointed as I am. I go alone on Sunday, feeling less hopeful. In the distance I see a girl with a stroller, but as she gets closer I see that it isn't her.

She said she wanted to be friends. Why hasn't she come back?

I keep watching for the girl all week, but I don't see her. On Friday, I walk to the park, but there's no sign of her.

I'm almost back at my house when I suddenly see the girl coming toward me with her stroller, clearly on her way to the park. I was too early! I'm so excited I start walking quickly toward her, wishing Ellie was with me. But when the girl sees me, she stops suddenly and turns to look behind her, as if afraid that someone might be watching or following.

"Hi! I've been hoping to see you!" I call. "Are you okay?"

"Yes. Okay." She speaks quietly, looking down at the sidewalk—not meeting my eyes. She may be saying she's okay, but she doesn't sound it. Her eyes are flickering anxiously and her fingers are clutching the handle of the stroller tightly.

"I went to the park a few times, but you didn't come," I tell her.

"Please—you must go," she tells me. "I must not speak with you here."

"Why not?" I ask. "What's wrong?"

She looks toward the house, as if she's scared someone will see.

"I'm sure they won't mind you speaking to me" I say.

She shrugs. I can see her shoulders shaking.

"What are you frightened of?" I ask gently. "Are you in danger? If you are, tell me and I can call the police for you."

"Please! No! No police! Go. Please go!" she maneuvers the stroller around me.

"Wait!" I beg, but she walks off quickly before I can stop her.

I want to go after her, but my legs won't let me. The walk to the park and back is as much as I can manage.

I am well again. I'm looking after the baby once more. I was taking him to the park—so happy to breathe fresh air. But the girl, Kasia, she was there, on the sidewalk—too close to the house. She wanted to speak to me—but I was so afraid they might see. I went quickly. I hoped no one saw me speak to her. The park was peaceful. Baby and I, we were happy there.

But when I return, Auntie is yelling and screaming about the nosy girl from across the street. She saw us. Why did Kasia come so close? Why can't she leave me alone? She puts me in danger—she knows nothing. She thinks she can help, but she can't. She can only make things worse.

Things are worse. Auntie told him, and he says I must go—and I know where he means. He's going to send me to work in the other place, where the sick girl came from.

She protests—she doesn't want me to go, and they are arguing. I know who will win. She is bad, but he is the boss. She has gone shopping and taken the baby with her. She has been out for over half an hour.

"Come," he says. "Get in the car now."

"Where are you taking me?" I ask in terror.

"You'll know soon enough—and you won't be coming back here."

"Should I pack clothes?" I ask, trying to delay. I have a skirt, two pairs of jeans and two tops, some ragged underclothes—that is it.

"You won't be needing them," he says.

His words freeze my blood. Is he taking me to the other place—or is he planning to kill me?

I get in the car, but she comes back and starts shouting at him. She wants me for the house and the baby. He is angry that she is making a scene. I look up in the window opposite. I wish the girl, Kasia, was looking out now—was witnessing this. If he takes me, I will disappear like a wisp of smoke. Kasia will never know where I've gone.

Now she is in the car—and the baby, too. They keep shouting at each other as he drives. We turn into a road and he slows down at a house. I know in my heart this is it. This is where that other girl lives and more girls, too. This is where most of the girls they bring for better life, jobs, education in this country—this is where they end up. I am the lucky one—or I was.

He has the car door open and is beckoning me out.

"I have a better idea," she tells him. "Deal with that girl—that

nosy girl. Teach her a lesson. She's the cause of trouble—not this one. This one I need. The baby needs."

The baby has started to wail, as if he knows what is happening.

"Shut him up, can't you?" he demands. But she can't.

"Let me," I say, and I touch the baby's hand—speak soft words. His big eyes look at me, his face striped with tears. But the screams turn to sobs. At last he smiles and then closes his eyes.

They are both quiet. My fear floods out to fill the uneasy silence.

"Okay, have it your way," he tells her. "A little accident, perhaps? I will enjoy teaching that no-good girl a lesson."

He gets back into the car and turns it around, and we are driving away again. I look at the sleeping baby and stroke his dark mop of hair. I tell him in my head how he saved me. He saved me.

I am to be saved—but what about the girl across the street? What about Kasia?

26

It's Mom's forty-fourth birthday. Dad suggests we have a BBQ lunch. Mom invites Devi, who is vegetarian, so Dad gets some veggie burgers. She asks Mrs. G. and Nav, but Mrs. G. isn't up to it—she's finding the hot weather hard to cope with. Nav can't come, either—says he's *busy*. Dad is taking the kitchen chairs and folding table out into a shady spot in the back yard.

Ellie texts me while I'm sitting in the kitchen. I've told her about seeing the girl. She wants to know what I'm going to do. I text back: I'm not sure.

Dad picks up another chair from the kitchen, and we follow him outside. "Nothing from that godforsaken son?" he says to Mom. "He couldn't even be bothered to send his mother a card. That's what he thinks of us. You are deluded, Anya, if you think he cares an ounce."

Mom shrugs. I know she's disappointed not to hear from Marek. I'm surprised he hasn't even sent a text or a WhatsApp message.

Devi arrives, which is a relief as Dad stops going on about Marek and instead starts talking to Devi about her online business. She sells bags and accessories online and is making a small but decent living doing it.

My phone buzzes. *Maybe you should call the police,* Ellie's texted.

I don't know, I reply. *She was so definite that I shouldn't involve them. I want her to trust me. She's free to go out, so it's not like she's a prisoner.*

I think she wanted to talk, just not there—not so close to the house, I text next. *Are you free later? Let's go to the park again. Maybe she'll come.*

"Put your phone away, Kasia!" Dad demands. "It's very rude."

"Sorry." I put my phone on the table. It vibrates immediately, but Dad is still watching, so I don't pick it up.

"I've been telling Anya she should do the same with her cakes," Devi says, still talking about her business. "She is a superb baker, as we all know."

She points to the birthday cake—a lemon sponge with cream that Mom has made.

"You could, Mom!" I tell her. "You could totally run a cake business!"

"It's in her family," Dad comments. "But I'm not sure Anya would know where to start. How do you sell cakes online? You can't just put them in the mail!"

"You'd have to market yourself on local websites, and that kind of thing," Devi explains to Mom. "Then there'd be a lot of word of mouth. I'll help you if you're interested?"

"It would be a dream to do that," Mom says, nodding. "To spend my days baking and have people paying for my cakes! And if I can work here, I can care for Kasia, too. But I can't see it as a reality."

"You should try, Mom," I say. "What have you got to lose?"

"I'll think about it," Mom agrees. She reaches for a knife to cut the cake.

"Wait!" Devi exclaims. "Where are the birthday candles? We have to sing, and you must make a wish as you cut."

"I'm too old for all that," Mom protests.

"No, you're not," I tell her.

I'm not sure if we have any birthday candles, but I go inside, search the drawer and find one. Then I have another hunt for some matches.

Dad is getting impatient.

"Can't we just eat the damn cake!" he calls.

"Patience, patience," Devi teases.

At last the candle is lit and we all sing, Dad imitating an opera singer and making us all laugh.

"A triumph," he declares, as he tastes the cake.

The house is stiflingly hot. I want to see Kasia. I need to warn her that she is in danger.

"It's so hot in this house, should I take baby to the park?" I ask.

"No—you are not going out today," she says firmly. "You are right. It is hot. I will open some windows."

She comes with a key and opens the narrow top windows. The tiny key glints as she turns it—as if it is speaking to me. Where does she keep this key? If I could find it, could I escape? Could I go and warn Kasia? Would I dare?

She puts the key in her pocket. I have no chance of retrieving it there.

I sit on the sofa and hug the baby, snuggling up as we watch cartoons. He wriggles away—he is too hot for hugs, and the high open windows are letting in only more hot air. But I need the comfort. I am afraid—afraid for Kasia. They want to stop her interference—teach her a lesson.

I want to push the door open and beg and plead with him—tell him to take me to the other house, but not to hurt the "nosy girl." But if he knows I am eavesdropping I will be punished—locked in the basement as he has done once before. And if he decides Kasia should have a little accident, it will happen, and I cannot stop it.

If I am quiet, maybe there is something I can do. I go back to my room and look out of the window, across the street. I hope to see her—to see a light on in her room, to warn her somehow—but her house is in darkness.

27

The next morning, a package arrives from Poland. I recognize Marek's writing right away.

"Marek didn't forget!" I tell Mom. "It's just a day late."

Mom smiles and opens it eagerly. She gasps when she sees what he's sent. It's an old scrappy-looking hardback notebook. She opens it, and I can see it is full of writing, in Polish.

Mom holds it to her nose, which seems like a weird thing to do with a book. Then she hugs it close to her chest and tears prick her eyes.

"It's my mother's," she whispers. "All my mother's wonderful cake recipes are in here. I've tried to reinvent them from memory, but here are the real recipes. Where on earth did Marek find it?"

She eagerly opens the accompanying letter.

"Aunt Maria found this at the back of a cupboard, and I thought you might like it," Mom reads Marek's words aloud.

"She said she never uses it. I'm sending it to you for your birthday."

"Something he didn't have to pay for—how is that a real gift?" Dad asks Mom.

Mom shakes her head firmly, and begins to leaf through the book. "Marek knows this book means more to me than hundreds of dollars—and now that I have it, maybe I will do as Devi suggests. It is a sign! These are the most amazing recipes. It is a precious, precious gift, Stefan."

Dad tuts, but he doesn't argue.

"Now, which should I make first?" Mom mutters, flipping through the pages.

"I don't know!" I tell her. "I'll leave you to decide—I'm going on my walk. See you soon."

He is going out in the car. I can see the expression on his face as he kisses her goodbye. What can I do? While she is in the kitchen, I dare to search their bedroom for the window key. This is a huge risk, and my heart is pounding with fear as I search. But I cannot find it. I do find something—an empty notebook with a pen attached. I could write a note—but how could I get it to her? It is such a short distance, but I have no way to get a note to the house across the street. I tear a page carefully from the notebook and take the pen—just in case—and on my mattress, I sit and write the note. I am not used to writing in English, but I try.

If she looks out of the window, I could hold it up but she would be too far away to read it. If I stand on a chair, I could push it out of the top window. If she was watching, she would see that I was trying to send her a message and come outside and pick it up. But maybe she is safer to stay inside—where he cannot get her. I stand by the window, the note tucked in my jeans pocket.

Then I see Kasia's front door open. She's coming out—and I pull the note from my pocket, wave it in the window, hoping the flash of white paper will catch her eye. But she does not look up. She is walking away down the sidewalk. Maybe she goes to the park in search of me. But she does not turn right. She is going to the stores or somewhere else. She is out on the street and in danger.

Maybe I am wrong. Maybe his threat was a pretense. Would he really do something so bad? I stay here, in the window, waiting for her to return, waiting and waiting even though I should be cleaning the floors. I want to see her come back safe.

Then I hear a door bang and see across the street that the boy who lives next door to Kasia has come out. I wave the note once more. He glances up and sees me! I hold up the note, press my nose against the window, my mouth making the shape of "Help" over and over, though my voice stays silent. I dare not call.

He looks puzzled. I stand on the chair—quickly, before he turns and walks away, I push the note out through the small window. He is watching! He is still watching as it flutters over the bushes near the front step. He hurries across, searching for the note on the ground. He is so close to the step.

I hold my breath.

He has the note! He walks away from the house as he reads it. Then he starts to run.

28

The weather is still hot today, and I feel sticky, but I'm glad to be outside, where at least there is a slight breeze. I was going to go to the park, but it's too much effort to walk in this heat, and I decide to go to the café, where there is air-conditioning. I'm happy that I can do this now—choose to walk to one place or another. And I am walking a little farther each week, too, without feeling worse.

The café is busy today, and I can't get my usual table by the window. I manage to find a space with a partial view of the street. I sit and have a cooling pineapple juice and watch the people going past along the sidewalk. Everyone seems to be in a rush today. Being still so much of the time has made me realize just how much time people spend hurrying around, with never a chance to think. I have plenty of time to think—maybe too much.

Then I see someone familiar. It's Nav—walking past, like he's on a mission. He's wearing denim shorts and a dark green T-shirt. He pauses, taking a step back and glancing in at the window—looking at my usual table. Could he be looking for me? Probably not, though I wish he was. I wish he'd turn and see me, but he doesn't. Seeing him this close makes me ache for his friendship. I decide I need to try one more time to make amends—maybe he'll respond if I see him face-to-face.

I hastily gulp down the rest of my drink and head to the door. In my rush, I knock a cup on the next table and some coffee spills over the top. By the time I've apologized and am out of the door, I can't see Nav at all.

The street seems eerily quiet now. It's weird how that happens sometimes—one minute there are so many people and cars, and a few moments later, no one.

I start to walk toward home, and then I hear a voice calling my name. Nav. Is it Nav? As I turn to see, a car screeches behind me. I look back sharply to see it swerving onto the sidewalk! Silver metal is coming right at me. I step back in horror, trip, can't get my balance, and the car's still coming.

From behind, someone pushes me sideways so hard I go flying. And then I'm on the ground, I feel the sting as my hand scrapes the concrete. There's a scream, a thud, and a surge of exhaust fumes that burns my throat as a roaring noise hits my ear. Then silence.

I dare to open my eyes, try to lift my head, but my vision

is fuzzy for a moment, and, by the time I can see, the car is a speck in the distance. I'm lying on the sidewalk. To one side of me I can see bare legs, brown skin. Someone is lying close to me, still—too still. I lift my head to see denim shorts, a green top, a familiar tousle of dark hair. Nav.

"Nav!" I yell. "Nav! Are you okay?"

I'm scared. He seems so still. I try to sit up, relieved to find I can move, and crawl nearer.

"Nav! Nav!"

Then my view is blocked. A woman is standing over me, and I see another kneeling by Nav.

"What happened? Are you okay?"

"A car," I croak, "did you see? It went on the sidewalk. Nav—he must have seen it. He pushed me out of the way, and I think it hit him."

"You just lie still. I'm calling an ambulance," she tells me.

But I'm trying to sit up. "Nav! Nav!" I cry. "He isn't moving!"

"Please lie still," she says. "My friend's a nurse. She's checking him out."

So I lie there, not moving—and we wait. A crowd gathers, but there's no one I know. I've no sense of how much time passes—it feels like some kind of weird dream. The ambulance comes. The paramedic checks me over and helps me to stand. I am relieved to find that I can. I have cuts and grazes, bruises, but I am okay.

"I saw what happened," I hear someone say. "It was going straight for the girl. That boy leapt in and pushed her out the way."

They have a blanket. They're putting it over Nav. Is he dead? Are they going to cover his head?

"Nav!" I yell.

"Hey, hey—he's unconscious," says the paramedic.

"Will he be okay?"

"Let's just get you both to the hospital," she says firmly. "I want you to be checked over thoroughly and then the police are going to want to talk to you."

I hadn't noticed the police until now, standing back talking to the other paramedic.

I don't think I need to get looked over, I feel fine, but I don't argue because I want to go with Nav in the ambulance. I struggle with the seat belt as Nav is strapped to the stretcher. I pull out my phone to call Mom as the ambulance starts up and I tell her to tell Devi.

Mom gasps and swears in Polish. "I'll be there as quickly as I can," she tells me.

I watch Nav all the way to the hospital. He doesn't move or wake up, and when we arrive he is whisked away. My legs give way as I try to stand, so they bring a wheelchair for me. I'm sure my legs aren't injured, but they are throbbing, and I know I can't walk another step today.

I am brought to the emergency room, still trying to

process what happened. Hit-and-run. That's what it was—deliberate—the driver came straight for me. But why?

Mom is in tears when she arrives, and I tell her what happened. I am checked out—and have to explain about my ME when the doctor wonders why I am finding it hard to stand. They say I can go home, but I want to wait, to find out if Nav is okay.

"Devi will keep us informed," Mom tells me. "Let's get you home."

An officer asks me questions before we go—not that I can tell him much. The car was silver. It came right at me. That's all I know.

I tell the officer about the silver car I saw out of the window that time, the man who seemed to drag the woman into it. But he says that silver is a very popular color for cars, and it's not likely to be connected. Of course, they never found any proof of an abduction, so it's not really any help.

It feels like hours before Devi calls to say that Nav has woken up. He has severely bruised ribs and a concussion, they're not sure how bad, but he can't remember anything about what happened.

"They're keeping him overnight," Devi tells me, "just as a precaution, because of his head. If it all goes well, he should be able to come home tomorrow. I told him what I know, and he's asking for you. Demanding to see you!" she says. "I didn't know you two had made up."

"We hadn't, but he saved me," I reply. "He saved my life. Can I come and see him?"

"Tomorrow," says Devi. "Wait until he's home. I think it's best for you both to rest today. You and Nav have been through a terrible ordeal," she says. "I hope the police manage to track that car down and get that idiot off the road."

"Yes," I say. "I hope Nav is okay. Tell him I'll see him tomorrow."

29

The next day I feel a little battered after being flung to the ground, but I'm relieved that apart from that I don't feel too bad. As I get dressed, I hear a car and look out to see Nav getting out and walking awkwardly up the path with Devi. I want to go next door right away but Mom insists I give him an hour or so to settle back home.

Later on, Mrs. G. lets me in. "Are you okay, Kasia?" she asks. "I am so shocked by what happened—so relieved that you and Nav are both alive and not badly hurt. Nav is in the garden—you can go to him."

"Is he out gardening?" I ask.

"No—resting outside and admiring his handiwork. The garden really is looking wonderful."

Nav is sitting on a plastic chair, facing the garden. He turns his head slightly and grins as I come outside. It's that old familiar Nav smile from before, and it warms my heart to see it. I realize just how much I've missed him. Devi said he couldn't remember what had happened with the car, and I wonder for a moment whether he's also forgotten what I said to him—how I upset him. I'd be glad if he had forgotten that.

"You've transformed it," I say, sitting down beside him and waving my arm toward the flowerbeds.

"Not bad, is it?" He beams. "Needs a lot of water in this heat, though. It's a shame Nani doesn't have a sprinkler system."

"Oh, Nav—you saved my life! Thank you!" I can't help blurting out.

"S'all right," he says, looking a little embarrassed.

"You were nearly killed," I say. "It was very brave."

"It's all a blur," he tells me. "I don't even remember where I was going."

"That car coming at me—it's another weird thing," I say, "like the girl across the street. She's real, you know? I spoke to her."

"The girl across the street," he repeats, looking puzzled.

"You remember I told you about her—and we knocked at the door, but no one answered? I kept seeing her in the window, but she never came out, and then I saw her at the park. The people there, they say she's their niece, helping out with the baby, and that she's eighteen, but she always looks terrified, and I'm certain she's much younger than that. I've been worried about her all this time," I tell him.

"That girl... My brain's trying to tell me something," he

says, rubbing his head. "It's a memory, something to do with yesterday, to do with that girl. I'm trying to think—I'm sure it's important, but I can't remember..."

"Did you see her?" I ask him. "She sometimes looks out of the window. You saw her once, remember—you told me."

"The window?" he repeats. "The window."

I can see he's thinking hard. I want to press him I'm desperate for him to remember. But I try to be patient. I look at the flowers, listen to a bird singing.

"It's no good," he tells me. "I'm sure it has nothing to do with that car that came for us, anyway."

Devi sticks her head out of the kitchen door. "Just putting your clothes from yesterday in the wash, Nav—I found this in your pants pocket. There's something written on it—I don't know if it's important? Anyway, here it is, in case you want it."

Nav takes the piece of lined paper and examines it. "I'm not sure what this is," he says shrugging. "It doesn't look like my writing."

He pauses, then looks up suddenly. "Hold on, I remember!" he says. "Kasia, it's coming back to me. It wasn't me who saved you, it was the girl—the girl at number forty-eight!"

"What do you mean?" I ask, wondering if his head injury might be more serious than anyone thinks. He isn't making sense.

"I came out to go to the store for Nani," he tells me. "I was about to cross the street when I heard a tapping sound, and it was the girl at number forty-eight, at the window. She was mouthing something frantically, but I couldn't make out what. Then she dropped a piece of paper out of the window—and it was this note."

He gives it to me. I read it, feeling goose bumps break out all over me as I see what it says. "Kasia—you in danger. They want hurt you."

"How did she know? I don't understand," I say, partly to myself and partly to Nav. "How did she know it was going to happen?"

"What you told me about the girl—have you done anything that could have made the couple there suspicious?"

"No—well...yes, maybe," I admit. "I've asked the woman about her a few times—and when I spoke to the girl near the house, she hurried off as if she was scared of being seen. Maybe they *did* see."

"Maybe they were worried about what she may have told you. They wanted to shut you up," says Nav. "The girl must have heard what they were planning."

"And she scribbled that note," I say, "and threw it out."

"I know I panicked when I read it," says Nav. "I'd seen you go out, and I just ran up and down the street looking for you. When I finally saw you, it was almost too late. I was only just in time. I only got to you because she warned me."

"You both saved me," I say, shuddering.

"There must be something seriously wrong in that house," says Nav.

"I've been saying that all along," I tell him. "It wasn't the man's car, though."

"Maybe he got a partner to do it," says Nav. "His car would have been too obvious. We should call the police. It was attempted murder!"

"But she said no police. She was terrified. They're dangerous people, aren't they? We've seen that today. We need to be very careful. If we speak to the police, we may make things worse for her."

I turn the crumpled paper in my hand, staring down at her words. Then I see on the other side, she has written in tiny writing: "Help me please."

"Look," I whisper. "She does want help. She's asking us."

"Show me." Nav takes the paper and peers at the writing.

"We have to do something," I tell him. "She got a message to us—now we need to get one to her."

It did not work. I tried and I failed—I failed so badly. Now two people are harmed, maybe dead. That poor boy—I sent him into danger. What was I thinking? I heard the car, the screech, I looked out—and I saw, far along the road, the two on the ground. That poor girl Kasia. Is she dead? I could look no more.

I am panicked. I cannot stay here with these mad people who will kill a girl on the street for trying to be friends with me—for caring. I must leave.

She is out. I am alone with baby. I put their clothes in the washing machine. This is what she was wearing yesterday.

I saw her put the window key in her pocket. I feel for it frantically, but it is not there.

The washing machine whirs and I go upstairs, taking baby with me. I will search once more for the window key. It must be somewhere. I know she has the front door key with her, but I believe the window key is here in the house. I must be brave. I search their room—every corner, every container.

I think it is nowhere. But then I find it. The tiny silver key glints at me from a small clay pot, a pot shared with pennies and paperclips. This is it. This must be it. I can open a window and I can go—I can leave.

I feel an urgency—I should not wait. But I cannot leave the baby here alone. I will have to take him with me. But no—he is not mine to take! She does not deserve him. She does not care for him like I do. He is safer with me. He will want to be with me. Then I must get not just myself, but the baby out of the window—and I will need the stroller, too.

I must move fast, and carrying him will be slow and difficult. They could come back at any time. I put baby on the floor, where he kicks his legs and watches me. I turn the key in the front downstairs window. It turns. It clicks. Now I could open it—I could open the window wide and be out.

But where would I go? Kasia, the girl, she is maybe dead or in the hospital. Where can I go? I have no one, nothing. They will find me and bring me back—punish me.

Baby has started to cry. I turn the key once more, locking the window. I put the key back in the pot, beneath the pennies. I sit on the floor hugging the baby, and, as I sob, he puts his chubby arms around me.

30

Nav and I wait the next day for the man and woman to go out. We are next door, and Nav is watching from his window but being careful not to be visible. The man goes first at half-past eight, but the woman is still there at 10 a.m.

"It's just our luck," I tell Nav, "I bet she'll stay indoors all day."

But then the door opens and she finally leaves, taking the baby with her. She locks the door behind her. The girl is alone.

"I think she's locked her in," says Nav. "If she can't open the door, what can we do?"

We go anyway. I ring the bell. No one comes. I lift the mailbox flap and call through. "Is anyone there?"

We wait. I call again.

"She's not coming," I tell Nav.

But then suddenly my view of the empty hallway is blocked, and two frightened eyes meet mine from the other side of the mailbox slot—so suddenly and so close that I jump back in alarm. The mailbox snaps shut.

It's the girl. She's really there. I lift the mailbox flap tentatively again.

"We've come to help you," I tell her. "Can you open the door?"

"You are alive!" she whispers, sounding surprised.

"Yes," I tell her. "We're okay. Thank you, thank you for your note—for trying to help me. Can you open the door?"

"No. Door locked." Her whisper sounds so far away, even though I know she's only on the other side of the wood.

"What about the back door?" I ask. "Is there any way you can get out?"

"Window," she says, so softly I have to strain to hear. Then she speaks more. "I find key for window."

"You'll have to be quick," I say, hoping it won't take too long.

"I can find—I get it," she tells me. "I get key now."

She disappears and we watch the windows in the living room.

When she doesn't appear instantly I wonder if she's changed her mind and isn't going to come—but then she's there, her face appearing behind the net curtain, her hand reaching out to the window lock, the tiny key between her fingers.

"Quickly, come on. We'll help you out," Nav tells her.

I look around, anxiously. There's no one in sight. She's opened the window, but she isn't moving. I see tears prick her eyes. She is too scared.

"It'll be okay," I tell her, though I have no idea if it will.

"You have to be quick. Someone might come back."

"Come on!" I say. "Hurry!"

Nav holds out his arm and the girl hesitates, but then she clambers out. She leans on Nav, and I see that her hands are shaking violently.

He takes her hand, tries to lead her toward the road, but she's not moving.

"This is no good," she says. "They will find me. They will hurt me. I must stay. I must go back."

"No—come with us. We will help you, I promise," I say. "Come across the street to my house. It is only a few steps."

The girl's eyes widen with fear. "Not safe," she says. "They will look near here for me. They know you. I must go far."

"Look—there's a bus coming," says Nav. "Let's just get on that. At least we'll be away from here."

On the bus I sit by the window, and the girl sits, head down, beside me. She flinches as the bus moves off, and so do I, but I know her pain is different from mine. I glance at her, sitting next to me. We've rescued her. We got her out.

"I want to thank you," I tell her. She looks at me wide-eyed.

"Your note—you told Nav I was in danger. He saved me. That car would have hit me if it wasn't for you."

"I hear what they plan for you—'no-good girl' they call you. I think you are good girl. I know you try help. I want help you."

"Well, you did," I say, nodding.

"What's your name?" Nav asks gently.

"Reema."

"How old are you?" I try next.

"Fourteen. Fourteen. Is truth."

"We believe you," I tell her.

"And what about your aunt and uncle?"

"They not real aunt, uncle. Not my family. They tell you lies."

"What do you mean? Who are they then?"

"The man is friend of my uncle—my real uncle. He tell my uncle they bring me here for a good life and good school. They say I will help a little with baby and house, but when I come they lock me in there—I cannot go out. No school. No money. I work all day, clean house, look after baby, cook all food for them. Before I come, they say no cost to bring me here, but now they say I must work to pay for my journey."

"That's terrible!" Nav exclaims. "We must get you to the police. They will help you and lock up those people."

"No police!" the girl shouts, and other people on the bus turn to stare. "Take me back," she demands. "I must go back." She stands up as the bus pulls to a halt, and Nav has to hold on to her arm to stop her getting off.

"Are you all right, dear?" an elderly woman asks gently. "Is that boy hurting you?"

The girl doesn't answer, but she shakes her head. The bus doors close, and she sits back down, hiding her head in her hands.

"I must go back," she whispers. "The baby—he needs me. And the police—they will lock me up, too, or they send me back, and my uncle—he not want me."

The bus stops again, and suddenly she's up and running out of the doors.

"No—wait!" I call, and Nav and I jump off, too, following as fast as we can.

31

I can't run—the pain is intense, and my legs give way after a few steps. I'm not sure Nav should be running, either, with his injuries, but he does. We can't lose her now. I stop and stand, panting, watching Nav. He is shorter than the girl, but she runs awkwardly, and he is faster. He runs past her, turns to face her, and blocks her from passing.

Her shoulders are shaking as she sobs. I drag my legs, walking as fast as I can, determined to catch up. Nav is trying to calm her down.

"Please—don't cry," I tell her. "We want to help you. What do you want us to do?"

"Take me back—you must. Take me back. Now. Now. Now."

"Okay," says Nav. "If that's really what you want."

I open my mouth to protest. After all this—we've got her out, and now we're going to take her back? But we can't force her to come. And if we don't take her back, she's going to run off, and maybe we'll never find her. Who knows what would happen to her then?

"Come on," says Nav. "We can cross the street and take the bus back. If that's what you want."

She nods, and I see her shoulders sink down with relief. I hold out my hand, and she grips it as we cross the street. She continues to grip my hand as we wait for the bus. She keeps looking down the road, waiting to see the bus, and she's clearly getting anxious.

"Ten minutes," I say. "It should be here in ten minutes."

We wait in silence. I can't believe we're doing this.

There must be another way.

"We want to help you," I tell her. "Why do you want to go back? Isn't there something we can do?"

"You are kind, very kind," she says. "I know you are kind. I see you at window—I think, *kind girl*. But no one can help me. It is not possible."

I meet Nav's eyes, hoping he will have an idea—something to suggest that will reassure her.

A man walks past eating a burger, and the girl's eyes follow him intently. I hadn't noticed how thin she was until this moment.

"Are you hungry?" I ask.

"I am hungry always," she says. "Not much food—only, how you say? What is left."

"Their leftovers?" I ask, horrified. She nods.

"Very small," she says.

"I'll get you something," Nav tells her. "Look—we can go into McDonald's, over there. I'll get you a burger, like that man?"

Her eyes are wide. "I..." She is almost salivating. "I eat and then you take me back—yes?"

"Yes," says Nav, though he gives me a meaningful look. He's hoping, like I am, that we'll manage to persuade her to do no such thing. He turns to me. "You want anything?"

"No, I'm all right. Maybe get her a drink, too?"

We find a table at the back of the room. She's breathing fast and every time someone comes in through the door, she looks around anxiously. They couldn't find us here, could they? I want to say something calming, but I'm not sure what.

"I remember when I first saw you in the window," I tell her. "It's so long ago."

"I remember I see you," she replies. "I think you work like me—I never see you come out."

"The first time I saw you, I don't know if you noticed me at all," I say. "Something happened—out on the street. Do you remember? Did you see it? A woman was dragged into a car."

Reema's face seems to freeze. There's new fear in her eyes. "You see that?"

I nod. "I called the police—I told them to talk to you, too, but those people you were living with, they said there was no one else in the house, like you didn't exist. I think the police thought I was making it up."

Reema frowns. I've been speaking too fast, and I don't think she's following.

"The police didn't believe me," I tell her, slowing down my speech. "And no woman was reported missing or anything."

"She one of *his* girls," Reema says, covering her eyes momentarily with her hand.

"What do you mean? Whose girls? Are you saying you know her?"

"She run away from him, from the place—how you say? The no-good place where girls wait for men. They took her back."

"What? She's a...prostitute? Is that what you mean?" I ask.

Reema looks unsure. "He *make* them do it. They not choose this. He bring girls to this country. They think go to school or jobs, but he bring them here, to place not far where you live—and he lock them. It is a trick. I lucky one. She wants me—for house and baby. If not, maybe I go there, too, for men."

"But Reema—how can you think of going back when you know all this?" I demand, in horror. "When you are out and free and you could help those girls?"

"You not understand. These people—they are strong, clever, so much power, you know? No one listen to me. I speak to police—they kill me. They will find a way."

"But what about those girls who are being forced against their will, like the one the man dragged into the car?"

Reema closes her eyes tight and then opens them again. "I cannot help them. I must help myself. Maybe I tell police and they get sent back to their countries. Maybe they angry—they safer, better life here."

"Doing that though?" I say, in horror. "How can their lives be worse?"

"You know nothing," she says, shaking her head.

"You have to tell the police," I tell her.

Reema begins to cry.

I'm scared for a moment that she's going to run off again, and I won't be able to stop her, but Nav appears with a burger and a Coke.

While Reema is eating ravenously, I tell Nav what she's just told me. "It must have been the same car—the one that got that girl and the one that tried to hit me. We have to do something!"

He looks horrified. "I think she's talking about trafficking—people, kids and adults, being brought from other countries to be used like slaves. I heard something about it on the news. Let's try online," he suggests. "There must be an organization or something that can help."

We both get out our phones. I explain to Reema that we are looking for someone to help her.

My search for "trafficked children" brings up the National Center for Missing and Exploited Children. I click the link.

"Here—look, it actually says NCMEC helps people who

have been victims of trafficking," I say, showing Nav. "There a lot of information about it. I wish I'd seen it before."

"Why don't you call them now?" he says, "and let Reema talk to them?"

I nod. I turn to Reema and explain about NCMEC. "They're not the police," I tell her.

She looks very unsure, but she doesn't say no. As I begin to tap the number into my phone, she doesn't protest. I pray that I will get through quickly, and I do.

I explain the situation, and I'm put through to a woman called Megan who listens carefully, encouraging me to talk and speaking back with a gentle, soothing voice.

"Would Reema like to speak to me herself?" she asks.

I hand the phone to Reema, and she takes it. I can see her hand shaking as she presses it to her ear. Reema answers questions with one word initially, but then begins to say more. Finally, she hands the phone back to me.

"Kasia, can you tell me where you are?" Megan asks.

I tell her.

"Wait there," she tells me, "and I'll speak to social services and arrange for a social worker to come and meet you and Reema. She has agreed that I can tell the police, too."

32

When the social worker, Amanda, and a police officer arrive, we are all taken to the police station. Mom and Devi have been called and are on their way. Reema asks for me to stay with her while she is questioned, but Amanda explains that isn't allowed. She gently convinces Reema that she will be there to support her, and the interpreter speaks to Reema and seems to reassure her. She goes off with them while I wait with Nav in another room. The officer asks us questions, and we tell her everything.

"To be tricked and brought to this country as a slave," I say to the officer. "I still can't believe it could happen—on my street, where I live."

"What will happen to her?" Nav asks.

"If she wants to go home, we will arrange that. But if she wants to stay here, we will help her to apply for asylum. In the meantime, social services will try to find a foster family to look after her."

"Maybe she could stay with us?" I suggest. "I can ask my parents."

"That's sweet of you, but I think she'll need to go somewhere far from here, in a protected placement. Otherwise associates of the people who took her might threaten her and make her go back with them. And people have to go through all kinds of checks and training to become foster parents."

"Can we stay in touch—will you let us know what happens to her?" I ask.

"I can't make promises about that, but I will try," she says. "If you want to write to Reema, I'll make sure your letters are passed on."

We are left to wait for what feels like hours, but probably isn't. Nav plays on his phone.

At last, the officer brings Reema to say goodbye.

Reema still looks frightened. She doesn't speak. "I hope you'll be okay," I tell her.

She nods.

"Don't worry—you're safe now," Amanda tells her. Standing there, Reema looks thinner than ever, even more like the ghost I once thought her to be.

"I'll write to you," I say.

She doesn't seem able to speak. She says goodbye only with her eyes and then she follows the social worker out through the doors.

Devi brought Mom to the police station, and she drives us all back home as Nav and I tell the whole story over again. I am suddenly overcome by weakness and exhaustion. "I need to lie down," I tell Mom, as the car pulls up outside our house.

"I'll leave you to rest," says Nav, and he disappears quickly inside Mrs. G.'s house. He seems so eager to leave that I feel a surge of disappointment. I thought we'd become friends again, but maybe I was wrong. The front door closes, and I wish I'd said something—said I was sorry for the way I treated him. But the moment has passed.

I let Mom hold my arm as I struggle up the stairs and sink down on to my bed. It's been an extraordinary day, though I know that something good has happened because of it and that Reema is now safe. But I can't help feeling sad about Nav.

The next day I lie in bed, reading about child trafficking. The stories are appalling. Children brought to this country and sold for sex or enslaved for domestic work. I read accounts about different children who've been trafficked. There's even someone like Reema—a girl trafficked for domestic service and just locked in the house all the time.

Ellie comes over. We've been texting, of course, but she is bursting with questions. I show her the stuff online about trafficking.

"That's horrifying," she tells me. "I'd never have imagined something like that. You were so right to be suspicious! And you're talking to Nav again?"

I nod. "He saved my life."

"I'm glad you've made up," she says.

"I'm not sure we've actually made up," I admit. "I need to apologize properly. I was awful to him after the concert. I don't think he's forgiven me. And I really like him, Ellie."

She looks at me. "You mean—you *like* like him?"

I nod, suddenly realizing it's true. I can feel my cheeks going hot.

"He's a good guy," she says. "You'll have to speak to him."

I nod again.

Ellie glances at her watch. "I've got to go," she tells me.

"Where are you off to in such a hurry?" I ask.

It's Ellie's turn to blush.

"Do you have a boyfriend?" I ask eagerly. "Here I am telling you about Nav! What aren't you telling me, Els?"

"I have got a date, as it happens," Ellie says, but there's something weird about the way she's saying it.

"Who with? Come on, spill!"

But Ellie is quiet, not meeting my eyes, picking anxiously at her cuticles.

"There's something I need to tell you, and it's difficult," she says.

I can't think what she's getting at. I joke, "It's not Josh, is it?"

It's meant to be a joke, but she doesn't smile. "Oh, God, it's *not*, is it?" I say. I don't want Josh anymore, but this feels a little weird.

"It's not Josh," Ellie says. "It's Lia."

"What? You mean..."

"Yes," says Ellie. "She's my girlfriend."

This is a total shock. "But...I had no idea! You never said... So are you..." I hesitate—I'm not sure what the right word to say is. Should I say *gay* or *lesbian* or *bisexual*? Ellie speaks before I can decide.

"I don't know what I am, exactly, Kas. We just know we have feelings for each other—something more than friendship. I've never felt like this about any boy. But I'm scared. I don't want to be defined as anything. I just want to be myself."

She's crying now, and I feel awful.

"I'm sorry," I say softly. "I didn't know. I wish you could have talked to me. You've been so supportive to me, and all the time you had this going on in your head. And I haven't even asked you if you're okay, or what's going on with you!"

"I didn't want to bother you with it on top of everything else," she says, squeezing my hand. "I'm glad I've told you now, though."

"So am I. And maybe it's weird, but I've been a little jealous of Lia—thinking she was going to be your new bestie. I feel much less jealous now that I know she's your girlfriend!"

"I'm frightened, Kas," she tells me. "Scared it will all go wrong. And people are so insensitive, wanting to put labels on things."

"I'm sorry *I* did that," I say. "What does Lia think?"

"She says we both want it, so we have to go for it."

"And that *is* what you want, too?"

Ellie nods.

"Then go for it. Be brave. It probably won't last forever—that's what you told me, didn't you? How many people marry someone they were at school with?"

"You're right—we need to lighten up, just enjoy it. I'm glad I told you—I was scared. I thought it might be too much for you. I didn't want to lose you, Kas."

"No chance!" I tell her, and we hug.

I am so happy when Nav texts the following day to see if he can come over. I don't feel up to getting out of bed, but I manage to sit up.

"Can you believe it?" I ask him.

Nav nods. "We did the right thing, Kasia. I'm glad we did it. I only wish we'd done it before."

"I hope she'll be okay now," I say. "I hope she can get asylum or something."

We sit silently for a few moments, but it's not an awkward silence.

"Are you okay?" he asks. "You're back in bed..."

"I think it's the shock of everything," I tell him. "But I get over setbacks much quicker now. The strict pacing has really helped. I'm sure I'll be okay. In fact, I bet I'll be up and about tomorrow."

Nav nods again. Is that relief in his eyes? Like he cares—really cares? Or am I imagining it?

"I heard you were going out with someone?" Nav asks.

"What? I'm not... Oh, Josh? We only...we had two dates. It's over now."

"Good!"

I laugh. I'm sure I see a glimmer of a smile from him. Is he really glad that Josh is out of the scene? Does he actually like me...like that?

"Nav?" I say.

"What?"

"I'm sorry for how I was after the concert—for the things I said to you. I was feeling really bad, but I know that's no excuse. I didn't mean them—I promise you."

He says nothing for a moment. Maybe I judged this wrong. I'm asking too much.

"I got the message," he tells me. There's a brusque tone

to his voice. “I know you’re not interested in me like that. I know I’m too short for you—I get it. I never really expected anything more, but I was hurt.”

“Short?” I repeat. “What do you mean? This was nothing to do with you being short.”

He shakes his head firmly. “Oh, but it was—even if it was subconscious, Kasia. No girl wants to go out with a boy who is shorter than her. That’s just the way it is.”

“That’s silly, Nav! Maybe some girls think like that, but not me. I could say the same, why would anyone want to go out with someone with ME?”

“I don’t care about that,” he says with a shrug. “I like you. I like you as a person.”

“I feel the same about you,” I tell him. “Your height was never an issue.”

There’s silence for a moment. Somehow we can’t look at each other.

“Nav—I really am sorry about the things I said,” I say next. “I’d enjoyed the party so much, and I’d felt so normal—and best of all was being there with you. I was so disappointed when I relapsed, especially since it was two days later. That often happens, but it still feels like a kick in the teeth. I’d felt like I was starting to get back to the way I was before—that I might be able to go back to school soon—and then I was so much worse, and Dad was so angry, too. I lashed out at you. I didn’t mean what I said, and I’m sorry, truly sorry. Can you forgive me?”

"It's not easy, Kasia. You hurt me big-time. I can't make any promises."

"Oh—okay," I whisper.

I'm trying not to cry. I can't cry. I can't let him see how much it matters.

But then I see he's smiling. "But if my height really doesn't bother you, then I think we should give it a try, if you want to—go out with me, that is? Or even 'stay in' with me, when you're not up to going out. Whatever... That is the convenience of living next door to each other!"

"I'd like that," I say softly. "Yes, please."

33

Mom shows me an article in the newspaper saying six young women, believed to have been trafficked to this country as sex slaves, have been rescued. Three men have been arrested, including a man who, along with his wife, has also been charged with keeping a fourteen-year-old girl as a domestic slave. I can't help wondering about the baby. Where is he now?

"We're so proud of you, *moje kochanie,*" Dad tells me. "What happened to those young women was terrible, and you helped them."

The house across the street is empty. I don't know how long it will be before new people move in.

The couple at 43 have gotten engaged. We only know this because Devi has done a far better job of getting to know our neighbors than we ever did. They are having an engagement party, and they need someone to make the cake. Devi has recommended Mom. Mom is terrified. She said no initially, but Devi has convinced her to do it—she says they want a very simple design and are more interested in a cake that tastes good.

Devi then insists that she get some business cards printed to hand out. "This is the way word spreads," she assures Mom.

Mom is in the kitchen for hours. She won't let anyone come in. Then, at last, she calls me.

"Do you think it's okay?" she asks, doubtfully. "I had to use online tutorials to learn how to make the flowers."

"Mom!" I exclaim, looking at the white cake, decorated with lemon-yellow flowers and a gold band. "It's beautiful! They will be so happy!"

Mom smiles. "I didn't think I could do it. Just shows you what you can do if you try."

"And with the right encouragement," I remind her. "You wouldn't have even tried if Devi hadn't pushed you."

"True," Mom admits. "That Devi is a persuasive one. I think I need to do a real class—food hygiene and professional baking, or even a business class."

"I could look online—see if I can find one," I tell her, "when I'm back from my walk."

"That's kind. Thank you."

But when I come out of the house, I have another idea and decide to walk to the library. The librarian directs me to the folder of information about local classes. I find exactly what Mom is looking for at the local college. My eye is also drawn to a rack, where there's a leaflet from NCMEC. It makes me think right away about Reema. I must write to her. I've heard nothing about how or where she is.

The leaflet is about an open gardens event. I pick it up. NCMEC has an event where people open their own gardens to the public for a day and members of the public pay to go in. The money goes to the foundation. I think immediately about Mrs. G.'s garden. Nav has done wonders with it. Would Mrs. G. let him open it to the public? It would be amazing to raise money for the organization that has helped Reema!

I take the leaflet and knock next door on my way back, eager to show Nav.

"This looks great! I want to do it!" he tells me. This is no surprise—I knew he'd love to show off the garden. "Do you think anyone will come, though? I mean, people around here..."

"Let's call and find out what you have to do first," I say.

He phones right away, but comes off the phone looking disappointed. "It's too late to get into the program for this year," he tells me. "Maybe next year. I'll have that garden looking even better by then. And you'll be healthier, too—and able to help me!"

"It's a shame," I tell him. I'd been so excited about the idea and I don't want to wait a whole year. "Couldn't we do it anyway, just arrange it ourselves? We could still raise money for NCMEC."

"How would people know to come?" Nav asks doubtfully.

"We could put flyers through all the doors down the street," I say. "We can offer tea and cake, too—Mom could bake the cakes. I bet people would come."

"Maybe you could play the cello, too!" Nav suggests.

"I'm not sure—I haven't played for so long. But I could try..." I tell him.

"If Nani and Mom agree then, yes, let's do it!" Nav says, smiling. "It can be a practice run, and we can try to get in the main program next year."

I write to Reema. I tell her about the plan to open Nav's garden. I'm not sure how interested she'll be. I wonder if she'll even want to hear from me. Maybe it will just remind her of the horrible time she had here. I tell her how my health is improving, how I am able to walk farther and am planning to go back to school in September, starting with two mornings a week and building up slowly.

I send the letter to Amanda, the social worker, so she can forward it to Reema wherever she is. I'd love to get a reply, but I don't hold out much hope.

Two weeks later, a letter arrives for me.

To Kasia,

How you are? I am good. I am so happy you write to me!

I stay with nice family, and Amanda help me find one cousin I know living here. I see my cousin now—he is very happy to see me. I go to school soon. People helping me so I can stay in this country.

You save me. Without you I still be in that house, and only look at you from window, with bad life. No life. I am still scared someone will find me—lock me again. But I am far away.

Thank to you Kasia and your friend Nav. You are good people. I hope you have happy life. Maybe I will meet with you one day?

Reema

I show Nav. "I'd love to see her again one day," I tell him.

We work together on the flyer for the open garden. Mom is very enthusiastic and is busy baking cakes and putting them in the freezer. When the day comes, the weather is glorious—hot and sunny with a gentle breeze. I am standing in Mrs. G.'s garden, though I will sit down soon since I still get pain in my legs. I have to be careful, but I've built up my strength so that I can walk for fifteen minutes twice a day.

I know now that I can't control this illness, I can't fight it or beat it with positive thinking—even though it really helps to have a positive attitude. I have the best chance if I pace myself carefully, but I can't always predict how things will affect me.

I am enjoying being in this flower-filled haven, listening to people admiring what Nav has done. Lots of people are here, walking around Mrs. Gayatri's garden. She is sitting proudly at a table, taking money as people come through the gate—money that is going to NCMEC, to help children like Reema.

We didn't know whether people would actually come. But they have! Kath and John from 43 have come, the engaged couple who now want Mom to make their wedding cake next year. From down the street, a family we'd never met, Helene and Birou and their three young children have come. I can see Mrs. Gayatri has her eye on them, afraid they will step on the flowers, but they are perfectly behaved and far more interested in the cakes.

Ellie's back from her holiday in Spain, and she's here with Lia sitting on the new bench. They both look very happy. I can also see several people I recognize from the café. Dad is talking to a man I don't know, and Nav is telling a pair of older ladies the names of some unusual plants. I think I hear someone ask if he will do their garden. He meets my eyes and smiles.

"So nice," Mrs. Gayatri says softly. "I didn't think people on our street would come."

"But they have," I say. "They have."

"Maybe we make a friendlier street now—better neighbors," she says.

I nod.

"And you have done so much," she comments.

"This." She sweeps her arm across the garden. "And that

girl across the street. These are big achievements. You have made a difference to the world—even from your sickbed."

I smile.

"And my Nav, I'm glad you are friends again—maybe more than friends?" There's a twinkle in her eye.

"Do you mind...me not being Hindu?" I ask anxiously.

"No, I don't," she says. "I disapproved of Devi's boyfriend all those years ago not just because he wasn't Hindu, but because I thought he was bad for her. And so it proved—he didn't stick around. But I lost my Devi for far too long. I have learned my lesson. I will let my Nav make his own choices—and I know you are a lovely girl."

"Hey—how about some music?" Nav asks. "I've brought your cello out on to the patio."

I've had a practice, and I know I can't play for long, but I manage a few tunes, and it is wonderful to be playing again. People stop talking and gather together, listening. I enjoy the applause.

I am tired after the long day and have a day in bed. I post pictures of the garden on the ME Facebook page and explain about fundraising for NCMEC. I get lots of likes. I also write about Reema—but I do it as a story, without writing her real name. I say it really happened, though.

Dina replies, saying both these things are amazing achievements—especially for someone with ME, who is often housebound. She says it just shows what is possible—and she reminds me how I thought my life was worth nothing when things went wrong with Josh. "Life is not only about boyfriends and exams," she comments. "You make me realize that many things, even tiny things—can make our lives worthwhile. What you have done is not small, though. You have done something incredible for someone else."

I am relieved that, after a day in bed, I feel okay and am up and about again. My phone rings, and it's Amanda. She's happy for me to meet up with Reema. "We can't bring her anywhere near you," Amanda explains. "There may still be people around who'd recognize her. She may not be safe. Sometimes trafficked girls are so brainwashed that they run off to be with the people who held them captive. They think they are safer that way—and they fear the authorities here more."

"That's terrible," I say. "I hope Reema wouldn't do that."

"Are you well enough to travel?" Amanda asks.

"How far?"

"Maybe an hour on a train," she says. "I could meet you at the other end."

"I think so," I tell her. "I'll have to talk to my mom. Can Nav come, too?"

Mom is worried, but with some persuasion agrees that I can go. Nav says he can't come, because he's taken on too many gardening jobs for neighbors, and, anyway, he thinks it is right that I am the one to meet Reema. I enjoy the journey so much. Every little thing that I couldn't do when I was sick,

I appreciate now in a different way. Simple things like travelling on a train. Mom is hoping by this Christmas that I will be well enough for a trip to Poland.

Amanda meets me at the station and drives me to a café. I spot Reema immediately. She jumps up, looking so happy to see me. She's wearing jeans and a pretty top, and she has a healthy glow. She seems relaxed, not stiff and terrified anymore. After a quick chat, Amanda says she'll leave us for half an hour and come back.

"You look great," I tell Reema, when she's gone.

"So do you—your health better now?"

"Up and down, but right now definitely getting better," I say.

"I meet many good people," she tells me. "They help me much. I miss baby. I worry for him, but they say he has foster family, too—nice people. I still scared sometime—alone, in dark, or loud voices—but I go to school September. That is everything for me."

"That's good." I smile. "Your English is getting better, too."

"I want learn—very much," she says. "My foster mother very nice. She help me. And my cousin, too. Long time I wait for this."

I nod. "I wish I'd been able to help you sooner. All that time... Do you want to tell me your story, how you ended up there? I mean—I want to hear, but only if you want to tell me..."

"I tell you, Kasia. You are my friend—but my English still not so good. When I eight year old, my mother very ill. My dad work hard, but he also ill and we have very little money. He go to work in another place far away. When my mom die one year ago, my uncle take my brothers to live with him, but he not have much money. He say he has good plan for me—his friend will bring me to England for good life. I will go to school and also help family with baby. They will pay me good money I can send back to help my brothers. So I come here. I love the baby, I cook good food—but they not pay me, no school, locks on doors, much, much work in house. They say I am nothing. It is terrible life. I not eat with them, but wait when they finish and I must stand to eat in kitchen. They do not let me sit."

"That's awful," I tell her. "What a terrible thing to do—they completely deceived you."

"I lucky, maybe." She shrugs. "It is better I care for baby and not have to go with men. Some girls not so lucky."

"But you saved those girls, too!" I remind her.

"I hope they happy," Reema says, nodding. "You visit me again?" she asks.

"Yes—if you like, I'd love to keep in touch."

"I want very much. You good friend to me." She wipes her eyes and smiles.

34

Mom has had three orders for cakes following the open garden day and is busy baking. I go next door to see Nav, but he is out with Devi, and I sit instead with Mrs. Gayatri for a while and talk.

"The open garden day was wonderful," she says. "I know the idea was yours—thank you so much. And I am so happy that your health has improved so much."

"So am I," I tell her. "I still have to be very careful not to overdo it. I hope I'm going to be able to cope back at school. I'm getting better now, but I might get worse again. You never know with ME. I'm worried—but I'm also happy."

"Yes—you must be careful, but you are so different from when you first brought that package to me."

"Your life is so different, too," I point out.

She smiles. "Yes—I just had the birds to keep me company then," she says, nodding. "I am so happy to have Devi back in my life—and of course Nav, too. The stroke was a shock, but

I am much stronger now, and, if it hadn't happened, maybe I would still be alone."

She says she'll get Nav to knock for me when he gets back. I go home and I've only just taken off my shoes when the doorbell rings. I can't wait to tell Nav all about Reema. I open the door—and nearly jump in the air. I am so shocked. It isn't Nav. It's Marek!

"*Marek! Mom! It's Marek!*"

"Hi, sis!" he says, wriggling out of his backpack and dumping it with a thud in the hallway, before throwing his arms around me.

"Not too tight!" I tell him as Mom rushes out into the hall. She's swearing in Polish.

"Oh, Marek!" she cries.

He lets go of me and hugs Mom.

"I thought it was time to come home," he says.

"Come—sit in the kitchen. Have some cake! Tell us everything," Mom demands.

We sit and listen while Marek tells us funny stories and asks us what we've been up to. I tell him about the open garden and about Reema.

"So good that you're not stuck upstairs anymore," he says.

Mom tells him how her cake business is starting to take off.

"I'm so happy you are home," says Mom. "But what are you going to do now? Will you go back to college?"

"Mom—I don't want to," he says, shaking his head. "I hated it there. It wasn't right for me."

"Your dad won't be happy," Mom says, sighing.

"Will he throw me out?" Marek asks. "I know how much I've disappointed him."

"He wants the best for you, that's all," says Mom. "If you don't go back to studies, what will you do?"

"I know what I want to do," says Marek, "but I need to talk about it with Dad first."

None of us are sure how Dad will react to Marek being back and we all hold our breath in trepidation when he comes through the front door later.

Mom rushes out to greet him. He suspects something immediately.

"What's going on?"

"Look who's here!" Mom says softly.

Marek steps out nervously from the kitchen. I am right behind him.

"Hello, Dad," he says.

Dad stands openmouthed. For once he says nothing. He seems lost for words.

"I'm back," Marek tells Dad.

"What for?" Dad asks gruffly. "You're returning to college?"

"No." Marek shakes his head.

"What you back for then?" Dad demands. "Money?"

"No, Dad—I want to work with you."

"With me?" Dad is openmouthed once more.

"Dad—I know you'd like me to study, but I want to learn a trade and work with you at the same time, like an apprentice. Maybe plumbing or something like that."

"This is what you want?" Dad repeats, looking bemused.

Marek nods.

I am still tense, waiting for Dad to explode. I sense Mom is the same.

"Okay," says Dad, slapping Marek on the shoulder. "Then that is what you will do."

"Really, Dad?" Marek asks.

"Yes, son," says Dad.

Nav is here. I'm on a high about Marek being home. Nav is still on a high from the success of his open garden day.

"So many came—we raised money for such a good cause!" he says. "Maybe one day I will have a garden at the Chelsea Flower Show! What do you think?"

"Anything's possible!" I agree.

He smiles. Then he kisses me gently on the lips, and I feel a rushing sensation, as if the blood is suddenly whizzing around inside me.

"You know what? This has been quite a year," he says. "So much has happened that I never imagined—meeting

Nani, moving here, a new school, the garden." He pauses, then reaches out to touch my arm. "Good things, but ordinary things. But you—there's nothing ordinary about what you did. Even with your illness, you saved a girl from slavery."

I picture Reema—her sad face at the window and the contrast with her vibrant, hopeful eyes when I went to visit her.

Nav's hand is so soft on my arm.

"With your help," I whisper.

"Her life is so much better now," says Nav. His hand slides down and squeezes mine gently, "and yours is about to get better, too."

"You mean going back to school?"

"No—not that." He grins. "I mean because of the hot guy next door! I mean you and me—us!"

"Oh—*that*!" I laugh, and I lean forward and kiss him softly back.

I am not a ghost. I am flesh and blood. I am more flesh now that I eat good food. The ache of hunger inside me has gone. I am afraid but I have hope, too. I have good people—my foster parents, my cousin, my friend Kasia. I will work hard at school. I hope I can stay in this country.

When I saw Kasia in the window I thought she was like me. She thought I was like her. We were both inside the house—never coming out. We were hidden, our stories never told. But now our lives have changed—we see the light. Like Kasia, I am no longer a girl in the window. I am a girl of many windows and many doors, too.

AUTHOR'S NOTE

I have personal experience of ME/CFS, which started in my twenties and seriously affected my life for the next ten years. I still have to be careful, because symptoms do come back if I overdo it—but I value every aspect of the life I now lead, remembering a time when I didn't imagine I'd ever be well enough to get married and have a family.

According to an Institute of Medicine (IOM) report published in 2015, an estimated 836,000 to 2.5 million Americans suffer from ME/CFS, but most of them have not been diagnosed. Many people recover after a period of months or years, but others remain severely affected, with some bedbound for years. When I began to plan this book, I was shocked to see how little progress has been made in research as to the cause or treatment. Research in this area has been grossly underfunded. I hope more funding will be forthcoming, and that progress will be made to help all affected by ME.

ACKNOWLEDGMENTS

I want to start by thanking my family—and especially my husband, Adam, and our children, Michael and Zoe, who I love so much.

I feel privileged to be published by Egmont, which has looked after me so well! My editors Liz Bankes and Stella Paskins have been wonderful. I also have a brilliant agent in Anne Clark, who helped me to develop the beginning of this idea into something that could become an actual book and helped me survive the ups and downs of writing with a deadline (a new experience!).

Many people helped me with the research for this novel—and I apologize if I have left anyone out. In particular I would like to thank Iwona Olejniczak, Raj Shah, and Savita Kalhan for support with Polish and Hindu aspects; Action for ME, Jess Muxlow, Abbey, Michaela, and many other young people with ME who answered my questions and/or gave feedback on the manuscript; the NSPCC, the staff of which was so helpful; and Ann-Marie O'Keeffe for gardening advice.

I'd like to give a special mention to Jennifer Brea, whose film *Unrest* about her life with ME is incredibly powerful and from which I quoted at the start of the book. Anyone who wants to know more about life with ME should watch it.

I am also so grateful for the support of Janis Inwood, former librarian of Southgate School, and Southgate School beta readers Sofia, Nina, Cameron, and Naeemah; my Friday writing workshop members Angela Kanter, Jo Barnes, Vivien Boyes, and Derek Rhodes—whose constructive feedback and emotional support has been, as ever, invaluable. I am grateful too for the support of City Lit, where I began as a student and now teach adults who want to write for children and young people. It's a wonderful place to learn and to teach!

READ ON FOR A PREVIEW OF ANOTHER HEART-RACING THRILLER BY PENNY JOELSON

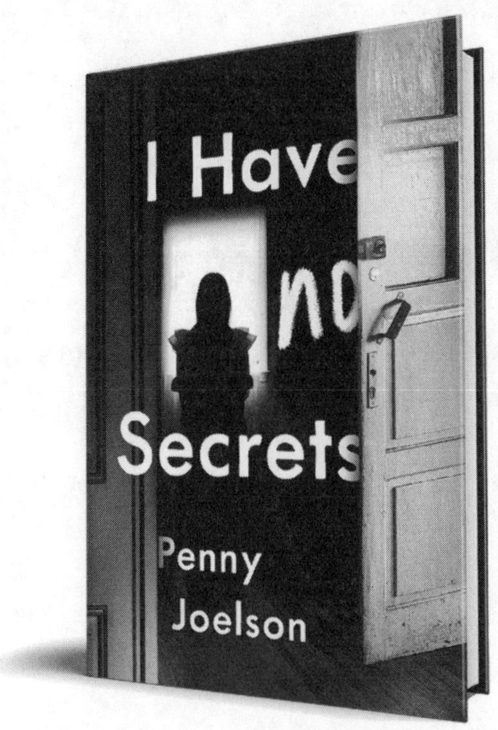

JEMMA KNOWS WHO THE MURDERER IS.

SHE KNOWS BECAUSE HE TOLD HER.

1

I tense up as soon as I hear the doorbell. I know it's him. I know it's Dan. Sarah's still upstairs getting ready, and I hope she comes down soon. I don't want him coming in here.

Mom calls up to Sarah, and I hear Sarah say she'll be down in a minute. "We've been keeping her busy, I'm afraid," Mom tells Dan, "so she hasn't had much time to get ready!"

"I know she wouldn't have it any other way," says Dan. "She's a gem—and you too. What you do for these kids."

I listen to them chatting away and Mom laughing at Dan's jokes. Everyone loves Dan. Then Mom says she has to get back to the kitchen—she's left things on the stove and she's sure Sarah won't be long.

It's quiet for a moment. I hear the distant clattering of pans in the kitchen. Then I hear Dan's voice, coming closer as he speaks.

"What show are you watching? Ah...*Pointless*!"

I can hear him breathing. Then he whispers, "A little like your life, isn't it, Jemma?"

He's standing behind me now, but I can't see him because my wheelchair is facing the TV. I try to focus on the game show questions and forget he's there, but he gives a long, dramatic sigh.

"Don't know how you can stand it." His voice is low, not loud enough to be overheard. "Watching television must be the most excitement you get." He only speaks like this when no one else is around. He used to ignore me completely, but not anymore.

He moves so he is in front of me, blocking my view of the TV. Grimacing, he leans forward. I get a gulping feeling, a tightness in my throat.

"If I were you," he whispers, "I'd kill myself."

My heart thuds as he rubs his head, feigning thoughtfulness. "Oh, yeah... You can't, can you? Listen," he continues, "if you ever want a little help, I could—"

We both hear footsteps on the stairs. Dan backs away. His face transforms from ugly sneer to fake grin, his features softening as if they have been remolded.

"I'd have done better than that couple!" he says, laughing and pointing to the TV screen. "We should go on this show, shouldn't we, Sarah?"

I get a waft of Sarah's perfume, which is quickly overtaken by the smell of onions frying in the kitchen. "I'm useless at trivia," she says, laughing as she comes into view. "I bet Jemma could do it, though, if she had the chance."

I don't know about that, although I do sometimes get the right answers. It's possible I'd be better than Sarah. She's an awesome aide, but she's not too smart when it comes to general knowledge—or boyfriends.

Out of the corner of my eye, I see her kiss Dan softly on the lips.

My own mouth suddenly feels dry.

The couple playing *Pointless* have been eliminated. They look very disappointed. Dan and Sarah only have eyes for each other. "Ready?" Dan smiles at Sarah. "You look stunning, babe."

She nods and turns to me. Her eyes are sparkly, her cheeks flushed. "Bye, Jem. See you in the morning."

"See you, Jemma," says Dan. He winks at me.

2

"Sorry to leave you so long, dear!"

Mom bustles into the room, and I'm relieved to hear her warm, soft voice. She switches off the TV and pushes my wheelchair into the kitchen, to my place at the end of the table.

I hear the car in the drive. Dad's back from taking Finn to his swimming lesson and picking up Olivia from ballet. Soon the kitchen is noisy and cheerful, as usual, and I push Dan out of my mind.

Olivia is boasting to Mom about how good her dancing was, and I watch as she shows Mom the new steps while Mom tries to get her to sit down at the table. She's nine and has only been here a year. We're all fostered. I've been here since I was two and so has Finn, who's nearly six. I've heard Mom say Olivia was "hard to place." Maybe that goes for Finn and me too, though Olivia's problems are different from ours. Finn is autistic, and right now, he is lining all his beans up neatly on the plate with his fingers. He's obsessed with straight lines.

Olivia is a whirlwind—sometimes a tornado—and she's loud. Finn and I don't speak, so life is very different and much noisier since she came.

"Sit down, Olivia!" Dad says in his "firm but kind" voice, and Olivia finally does. At least she doesn't start one of her tantrums.

Mom serves Dad's lasagna, then starts feeding me my mushed-up version. Dan's words creep back into my head while I'm eating, and I try to shut them out.

"*If I were you, I'd kill myself. Listen, if you ever want a little help, I could—*"

I can't believe he said it—as if my life is worth nothing!

Olivia is wolfing down her food like she's never eaten before. She's skinny, but she has a huge appetite. Finn isn't eating. He's still lining up his beans, concentrating as if his life depends on it.

"Come on, Finn," Dad coaxes. "Time to eat them now."

But Finn clearly doesn't think his line is straight enough.

"Finn, my love," says Mom gently, "why don't you start with the lasagna?"

I don't think Finn is listening to Mom, but I think he's happy now with his line of beans. In any event, he forks a small amount of lasagna into his mouth.

Mom spoons some more into mine.

"I saw Paula earlier," she tells Dad. "She looks dreadful, the poor woman."

"Still no news?" Dad asks. Mom shakes her head.

"News about what?" Olivia demands.

Paula lives down the street, and her son, Ryan, was murdered last month. He was nineteen, and he was stabbed to death, and no one knows who did it. Everyone's talking about it, though—it's even been on the radio.

Dad quickly changes the subject.

"Finn's swimming like a fish now," he tells Mom. "He's come along so fast."

"And I was really good at ballet!" Olivia says, never wanting to be left out.

"I'm sure you were," says Dad.

"How was school?" Mom asks Olivia. She shrugs.

Olivia never wants to talk about school. It's like it's some big secret for her.

I have no secrets of my own. I've never done anything without someone knowing about it. I'm sixteen years old, and I have severe cerebral palsy. I am quadriplegic, which means I can't control my arms or legs—or anything else. I can't eat by myself. I can't go to the bathroom without help. I can't move without someone lifting me with a hoist or pushing me in a wheelchair. I also can't speak.

I've been this way all my life. I can see, though, and I can hear. Sometimes people forget that; they don't realize that I have a functioning brain. Sometimes people talk about me as if I'm not even there. I hate that.

And sometimes people tell me their secrets. I think it's because it's really hard to hold a one-way conversation. If they are alone with me, they want to talk to pass the time and they end up telling me stuff. They know I won't tell anyone else, so they think telling me is safe. The perfect listener.

Sarah told me her secret. She's cheating on Dan. She's still seeing Richard, her old boyfriend, because he's so sweet and she can't stand to hurt him by breaking up with him. Neither of them knows the other exists. I'm always worried when Sarah has a boyfriend, although I enjoy the way she gossips to me about them. She has this dream of a fairy-tale wedding—she's even shown me pictures of her ideal wedding dress online. I know I should want her to be happy, and I do. It's just that I'd miss her so much if she went off to get married. She's the best aide I've had.

More than that, I don't want her to marry someone who isn't good enough for her. And I definitely don't want her marrying Dan.

ABOUT THE AUTHOR

Penny Joelson was born in London, where she still lives with her husband and two children and teaches creative writing. She is also the author of *I Have No Secrets*. Find Penny on Twitter @pennyjoelson.